Dawn's Web

Patrick Shattuck

Los Angeles, California USA

Acknowledgments

First and foremost, thank you to my lovely wife, Molly who tolerates my typing at five o'clock in the morning, and thanks to my brother, Frank who insisted I hone my craft so I didn't ruin the family name.

Thanks to Laura Italiano for helping me research the "Baby-Faced Butchers," and thanks to Brian McCabe for inviting me to read my first draft at Rocky Sullivans.

Thanks to Hailey Kline for perusing the pages with a keen and thoughtful eye, and endless gratitude to Leya and Steven Booth who made my dream come true by publishing this book.

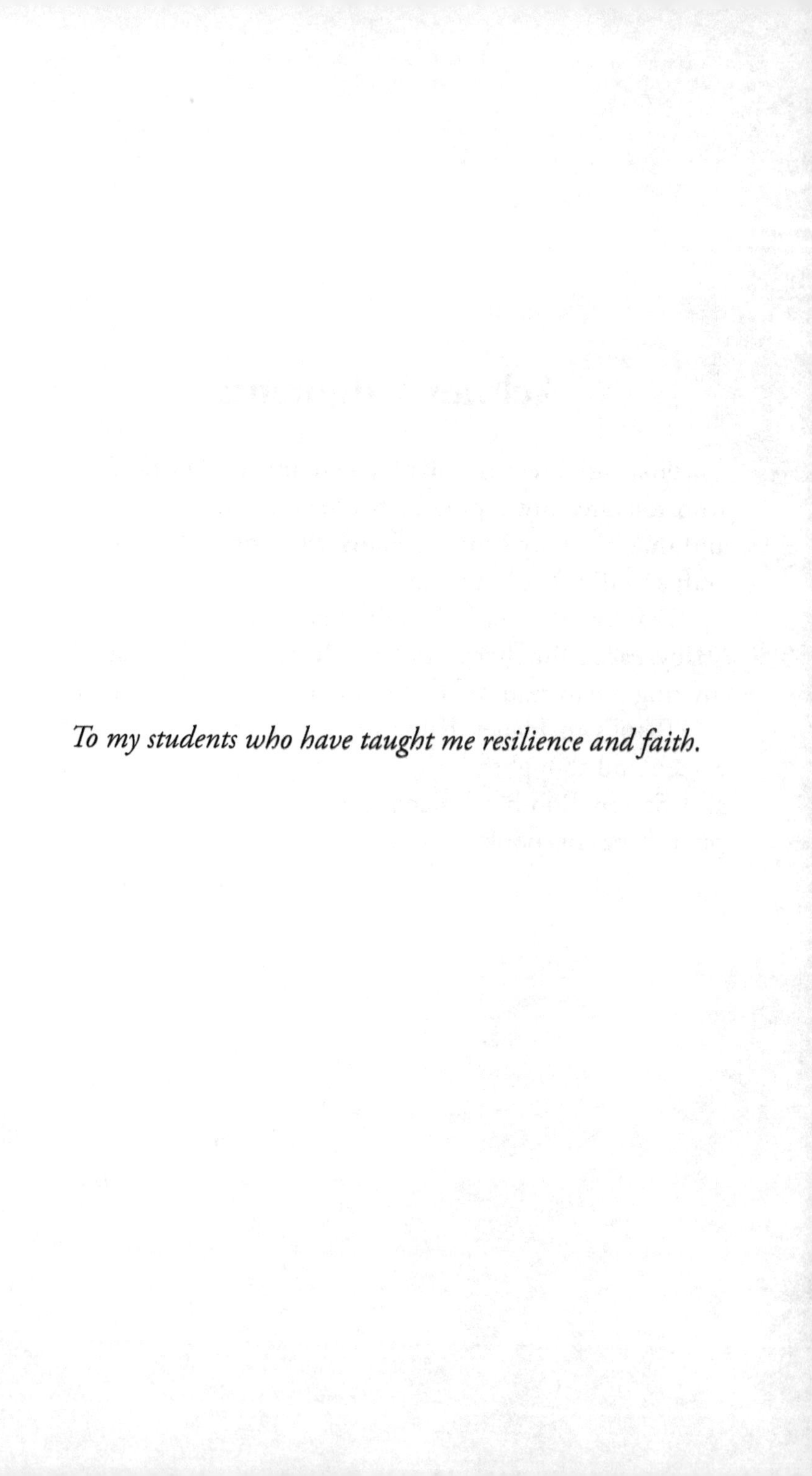

To my students who have taught me resilience and faith.

Dawn's Web

1

When morning finally broke into Mickey Miller's bedroom, it found a typical scene—empty beer bottles, the smell of stale bong water, and a powder-stained mirror on the table. However, there was nothing typical about this day because they were burying his mother in the Bronx later. Last week, while playing Monopoly Xbox with her forty-year-old son, Grace Miller had suffered a hemorrhagic stroke. While her brain bled, Mickey had collected his two hundred dollars for passing "Go" and bought another hotel. Assuming her lopsided smile and lifeless arms were signs of fatigue, he went out onto the fire escape, smoked another bowl, and went to bed. It wasn't until he found her in the same position the next morning that he figured something might be wrong.

Although Mickey's failure to respond raised some suspicion (for if he had called right away, Grace's chances of survival would have greatly improved), the investigation revealed no signs of foul play. Even after considering his myriad misdemeanors (including public intoxication, providing alcohol for minors, petty theft, and drug possession), police concluded that "Norman" (a nickname officers had given him denoting Hitchcock's famous "psycho") wasn't culpable in his mother's death. While the sobriquet may have been a crude attempt to mock the man-boy who still lived at home, it was a stroke of uncanny prescience, for within a few short months, Mickey would be the focus of a brutal murder that would shock and horrify even the toughest New Yorkers.

❧

Duncan Bright, a recently divorced Manhattan psychologist, labeled his clients' progress with different phrases, and a "Coming Out Party" was the day people chose to reveal themselves. Ironically, Zander and Dawn, his fifteen-year-old clients, had both chosen the same day to have their Coming Out Party, even though he treated them separately. In his experience, most clients, especially teenagers, went through a dormancy period at the beginning of counseling sessions where they stayed inside themselves. Most spent this time discussing trivial things, but Dawn, a beautiful girl with bright blue eyes, hadn't talked at all. For the first four sessions, she simply stared at the clock, looked at her phone, then stared at the clock again. At 3:30, she would pack up her things, put on her earbuds, and leave. Dr. Bright had had reticent clients before, but never one like this. Today, he decided to bring it to her attention. But as it turned out, he didn't have to.

"What's that?" Dawn said, pointing to the ceiling after a cacophony of power saws and hammers had shattered the silence.

"They're doing some work upstairs," Dr. Bright said, looking up, clearly frustrated by the noise. "But they're not supposed to work between the hours of nine and five."

"And how does this make you feel?" Dawn asked, adopting a condescending tone clearly meant to mimic his manner.

"A bit annoyed," he replied.

"Annoyed? Come on now, doctor. We can do better than that. Are you upset?"

Even though this was mindless banter, Dawn was at least talking now. He decided to play along. "No, I'm not upset."

"Liar," she said with a coy smile on her face. "You're upset with me right now."

"But why should I be upset with you, Dawn?"

"Because I'm a little bitch. You're not mad at the hammering. You're mad at me."

Just as Dr. Bright was about to reign the conversation back into the realm of reality, Dawn stood up, and walked out the door. Two minutes later, her mother called. Louisa Fontaine was a corpulent quinquagenarian with dark brown eyes and a nervous voice. Traces of her former beauty still resided in a face ravaged by cosmetic surgeries and prescription drugs.

"How is she, Doctor?" she asked.

"Well, Dawn's making progress, but these things take time, Louisa."

"Has she said anything about school yet?"

"No, not yet."

This past April, Dawn had stopped going to school. At first, she'd complained of headaches, but after the best physicians in Manhattan had said there was nothing wrong with her, she'd started playing hooky. This hadn't been discovered until Louisa, passing by her school one day, decided to pop in. When the headmaster told her Dawn hadn't been there in a month, she'd fainted, and had to be revived in the nurse's office. It seemed the clever freshman had swiped some of her mother's stationery and had written a note to the school saying she was going to England with her father and wouldn't be back for the rest of the school year. Where Dawn had been every weekday during the entire month of April was, in Louisa's words, "one of the unresolved things" Dr. Bright was "being paid to find out." Louisa, like so many parents of troubled teens, felt overwhelmed by guilt because her daughter had become an unpredictable, moody stranger. Deep down in her heart, Louisa blamed herself for the shift and the growing rift between them.

"Why is it taking so long, Doctor? She's been in therapy with you for four weeks," Louisa asked on the verge of tears.

"Well, Louisa, some people take longer to open up. You see, I'm still a stranger to her, and…"

"I'm not blaming *you*, Doctor. It's just that I don't see any progress, and you'd think that, after four weeks…"

Louisa came across as overbearing, but it was only because she perceived Dawn as a living symbol of her own neglect, and the quicker she could get Dawn's troubles straightened out, the quicker she could cut the vines of guilt that were strangling her heart.

∾

Zander was a pale, lanky, f-bomb dropping fifteen-year-old with fierce, dark eyes. He wore baggy pants and big t-shirts to hide the insecure kid inside him. Dr. Bright had met his mother, Sharon, an attractive blonde, several weeks ago when she had come into the office. Her visit had impressed the doctor because most parents of his adolescent clients were content with an initial phone call, but she had wanted to meet the person who'd be counseling her son. Furthermore, Dr. Bright had been struck by Sharon's candor when she had reflected on her recent divorce from a drug addict, and the tenderness that radiated from her pretty green eyes when she discussed her son.

Zander was supposed to come to Dr. Bright's office every Tuesday after school. Sharon had been picking him up and bringing him, but Zander, mortified by her presence at school, had promised he'd come by himself. After Dr. Bright had agreed that the boy's coming alone would be better, she'd acquiesced. That first Tuesday, he'd arrived twenty minutes late and swore he'd never be late again. The following Tuesday, Zander hadn't shown at all, so Dr. Bright had called his mother. Counseling teens came with added stress because if an adult missed a session, it wasn't a big deal—they either gave him twenty-four hours' notice or they still had to pay for the session. But if a teen didn't show, he was obligated to call the parent. Then, the parent punished the kid, and the kid came in the next week mad at him. Guiding teens through the choppy waters of adolescence could be very gratifying, but dealing with scenes like the one about to unfold in his office put gray hairs on his head.

"He promised me he'd come here every Tuesday, but he can't be trusted! Now, he's mad because I drove him here!" Sharon was gripping her purse so tightly her knuckles had turned white.

"Shut the fuck up, you fuckin' whore!" Zander erupted.

She burst into tears, and her son threw his hat at her.

"Okay, okay," said Dr. Bright, "Sharon, will you please come back at 4:30? And, Zander," he said, picking up the boy's hat, "please have a seat."

"Hey, gimme my hat back, man!"

"In a minute," the doctor said, as Sharon walked to the door like someone under anesthesia. "Come back around 4:30. Okay, Sharon?"

She paused in front of the door as if she'd forgotten how it worked, then opened it and walked out.

"Here." Dr. Bright threw the hat to Zander.

After getting him settled down, Dr. Bright made the mistake of asking the boy what he thought was the problem. Not that the question itself was a mistake; kids like to be asked, rather than told. It was Dr. Bright's inappropriate use of the word "problem," which should never be used with teens, because they don't see it as a term denoting inquiry or consideration. They see it as a rock hurled against their glass lives. As a result of the doctor's faux pas, Zander shut down, and after several failed attempts at communication, Dr. Bright stopped talking too, but the silence didn't faze Zander a bit. He looked around the office, checked his phone every few minutes, and fingered through the magazines in the rack beside him until it was time to leave. Then, at 4:30, he popped in his earbuds, gave the doctor a thumbs up, and left without closing the door. And although it was a small, perhaps unconscious gesture, Dr. Bright appreciated the fact his client hadn't closed the door because it symbolized his willingness to return.

ॐ

"How old are you, Doctor?" Dawn said, scanning his shirt and hair during their next session.

"Fifty-two."

"Fifty-two!" she screamed with a hand on her mouth. "You're older than my mother!" She laughed, and for the first time he saw the fifteen-year-old who'd been desperately trying to hide behind layers of thick, black eye shadow, tank tops that wouldn't fit Barbie, and push-up bras that made her 32Bs look like 36Ds. This contrast between Dawn's credulous eyes and her promiscuous costume made the doctor reflect on one of life's greatest ironies—the first thing teens do in their rebellion against adults is to act and dress more like adults. Meanwhile, their parents become surly and sullen—just like teens.

"So, Dawn, what happened last Saturday night?" Dr. Bright asked.

"Nothing." She pulled her knees to her chest, as if suddenly embarrassed by her premature jaunt into womanhood.

"Your mother said you threatened her with a steak knife," he probed.

She blew up laughing. "Well, you know she's completely insane, don't you, Doctor?"

"No, I don't know that, Dawn."

When Dr. Bright had originally heard about the incident, he was tempted to report it to the police, but Louisa had begged him not to because she had said that, aside from that scene, things had improved at home and police involvement would do more harm than good. The doctor had reluctantly acquiesced to her request; however, he cautioned Louisa that any more incidents involving potential harm would result in a police report.

"Well she is," Dawn continued. "Completely fucking insane. Do you want to hear the real story? See, she likes me to be the good little debutante, and go all these places with her. And I hate all these fucking places and these fucking people, too. Anyway, last Saturday night, some boring writer was reading from his boring book at the Ninety-Second Street Y, and I didn't want to go. So she flew into a rage."

"What kind of a rage?" the doctor inquired.

"First, she pulled the tablecloth off the table, and all the dishes went flying. Then, she screamed at my father 'cause he wouldn't take her side. Then, the fat whale came after me, and I just happened to be holding my knife from dinner. She jumped behind my father and screamed, 'Help, she's got a knife! Help! Help! She's got a knife.' Then she ran out of the room."

Dr. Bright pictured Louisa running out of the room and a spear of guilt went through him for not reporting it.

"Wait Doctor, I'm not done." Dawn was still laughing. "Then fatso locks herself in her room, and my father gets all worried and tries to break the door down. But he separated his shoulder trying, and made me call 911. But see, I didn't know who I was calling for. So I said, 'Come quick! My father broke his shoulder and my mother went insane.' But then I started laughing, and the operator hung up on me." She kicked at the floor with one foot to make the swivel chair spin around.

"What happened next, Dawn?"

When the chair stopped spinning, she looked at him absently, like an infant whose eyes rested on things without really looking at them.

"Dawn?" He slightly raised his voice.

Thoughts fell back into her eyes. "What would you have done if you had been there, Doctor?" she asked.

"I would have called the police."

Her eyes filled with venom. "You're so predictable, Doctor." She began gathering her belongings.

"Where are you going, Dawn?" Dr. Bright asked.

"I'm out of here." She put in her earbuds.

"Well, we still have fifteen minutes left."

"No," she corrected him. "My mom said I can leave when I want to."

Dr. Bright didn't believe for a second that Louisa had given her daughter permission to leave early, but he didn't want to challenge the girl at the moment, so he took a different route.

"Oh, okay. That makes sense," he said amiably. "But can I ask you a question before you go?"

She pulled out one earbud to acknowledge her acquiescence.

"Thank you," he said. "Why did you call me predictable?"

"Because you're taking my mother's side and that's what adults do," she answered.

"What do they always do, Dawn?"

"They back each other up and don't believe the kids." A frail tear formed in the corner of her left eye. Dr. Bright reflected on his own adolescence fraught with fears, inexplicable sadness, and the heavy feeling that the world was against him.

"Dawn, let's get one thing straight." He handed her a tissue. "I am here to help *you*. Not your mother or your father. *You*."

She held the tissue and looked at him as an incipient tear slipped down her cheek.

"Now, is there anything else you wanted to tell me?" he asked.

"Well, yeah, but," she smiled and pointed to her watch, and Dr. Bright realized that their time was up.

"Oh right," he said.

"Thanks Doc." She gathered her things, smiled at him again, and left.

☙

When Doctor Bright walked in the next morning, the red light on his telephone was blinking incessantly, indicating multiple messages. But before he had time to check them, Louisa called.

"Doctor, it's Louisa Fontaine. Have you seen Dawn today?!" Her voice leaped through the phone.

"Why, no. I saw her yesterday, though."

"Well, she never came home last night and we're worried sick. Did you say anything to upset her, Doctor?"

"I…"

"And don't give me any of that confidentiality crap! I want to know what was said!"

Suddenly, it sounded like two socks were fighting over the phone. Then, another voice emerged. "Doctor, this is Howard Fontaine. I'm terribly sorry about that."

"That's quite all right," Dr. Bright said.

"Is there anything you can tell us about yesterday that might help us find Dawn?"

"We spoke about the knife incident. But that's about it. Has she ever run away before, Mr. Fontaine?"

"There was that one time last April, but other than that, no."

Even though Louisa was hysterical, she seemed to understand, much more than her calm husband, the dangers awaiting a fifteen-year-old girl, especially one who looked like Taylor Swift, in New York City.

Dr. Bright encouraged Howard to call the police and report Dawn missing. He also urged him to tell them about the knife incident over the weekend as it would give police a better picture of the situation.

2

Evelyn, an obese attorney with jet black hair and violet eyes, assuaged her loneliness by inventing men. She had come to Dr. Bright three years ago after being fired from her law firm. Crippling anxiety had caused her to exceed the allotted amount of sick days, so the higher-ups at Sheering and Gleason had decided to let her go.

"So what do you think? The doctor or the lawyer?" she asked.

"I'm not sure, Evelyn. They both sound nice."

She invented one guy and talked about him for a few weeks. Then, she invented another guy and fretted over choosing between them. It had been going on like this for years. Aside from her mental issues, Evelyn had enormous talent. Multidimensional characters with different virtues and foibles came to life in Dr. Bright's office, and he really believed that part of her problem was that she should've been a playwright.

"See, Peter, the doctor…" She looked out the window. "Well he's nice, but there's that mother of his, and I'm afraid she'd always be between us."

Evelyn proceeded to tell Dr. Bright that Peter's mother deliberately called when they were having sex. And he pictured them having sex, even though Peter didn't exist. When Dr. Bright asked how Peter's mother could possibly time the calls, her eyes turned cold and he backed off, because tearing down an illusion has to be a slow and delicate process. Yet, when he tried to return to the fantasy, she made up a story about having an appointment downtown and abruptly left.

After Evelyn, Dr. Bright saw Brad. Well over six-feet tall with broad shoulders and blond hair, Brad resembled a movie star from the Golden Age of Hollywood. He had been a standout lineman for Yale, and was now making shoestring tackles on Wall Street for two million dollars a year. Brad crucified himself whenever he couldn't be the god in bed that he used to be on the football field. He had been struggling with frequent bouts of erectile dysfunction. Or, to put it more plainly, his penis had been uncooperative at inopportune moments. Even though erectile dysfunction is an innocuous, usually short-lived condition, most men would rather have the bubonic plague because of what it represents—namely, vulnerability and powerlessness. Two baneful words, especially to American men raised on Rambo and John Wayne. Interestingly, within the edicts of this macho mythology, psychotherapy is also perceived as a doctrine of weakness. By coming to therapy, Brad had already broken through one boundary. Now, all he had to do was drop that lexicon of this patriarchal paradigm. For instance, the whole idea of "losing" an erection.

"Brad, your penis can't get lost," Dr. Bright said.

"Okay, I didn't mean I lost it. I mean it went down."

"But, Brad, listen to that sentence: 'It went down.' You make it sound like your penis is in charge. Like it goes up and down when it wants to."

"But it does!" Brad cried.

"No, it doesn't," Dr. Bright replied, getting a slight headache. "Brad, is your penis attached to your body or is your body attached to your penis?"

"I'm not sure."

They both stared at the floor for a while.

"Doctor? Is my penis attached to my body or is my body…"

"Brad, you're one thing. Your penis is a part of your body and your body's a part of your penis."

"So, then we're both in charge?" the stockbroker asked timidly.

"No. There's no both. You're one thing."

"Me and my penis?"

"Yes!"

Brad wasn't the first guy to come to Dr. Bright because of a "lost" erection. In fact, a lot of his male clients had complained about the very same thing. He had tried telling each of them that these episodes were, for the most part, emotional reactions to something. But they continued to punish themselves.

Dr. Bright was awaiting his next session with as much enthusiasm as an approaching colonoscopy—because Zander had gone out last Friday night and hadn't returned until Sunday morning, Sharon had scheduled a "family meeting" that would exceed the doctor's grim expectations.

"I told ja a million times! I was with Dad!" Zander screamed, getting out of his chair.

"That's a lie!" Sharon stood up.

They faced each other for a few tense seconds and before Dr. Bright had time to intervene, Zander slapped his mother across the face. The force of the slap was innocuous; however, in her attempt to dodge the strike, Sharon tripped over her purse and fell face-first into a bookshelf. The next few seconds congealed like moments in a scary dream as Sharon collapsed and Zander ran out the door.

After calling 911, Dr. Bright started to put a pillow behind her head, but he stopped when he saw that the left side of her face had swollen to the size of a softball. Paramedics arrived first. After taking her vitals and asking a few questions they rolled her onto a stretcher, and took her away. Two officers arrived shortly afterwards. The doctor had expected them to ask myriad questions about Zander, but, after writing down a brief synopsis of events and getting a description of the boy, they departed, and Dr. Bright restored the fallen books to their places upon the shelves.

3

Winter had come early to New York this year, and the brilliant yellow leaves that usually brightened Mickey's window on Thanksgiving morning had long-since fallen, revealing the ghostly bricks of the pre-war brownstone next door. Adding to the gloom, this would be the first time that he hadn't awoken to the smells of turkey, stuffing, gravy, and his mother's homemade apple pie. The table that would have been set with linen napkins and antique China was now littered with a bong, a glass pipe, rolling papers, and a mirror. However, one item amidst the array of sordid equipment, a three-beam scale, signaled a turning point in Mickey's life. For, now that he was the beneficiary of his mother's life insurance policy and could afford large quantities of drugs, he had gone from buyer to seller, and this shift had given him something he'd been craving his entire life—status. Now, when he walked into the dives along Broadway and Amsterdam, people approached *him*, people bought *him* drinks, people sought *his* advice. And whereas before he had to settle for half-comatose whores to satisfy his lusts in bathroom stalls, he now had sexy, young girls performing all kinds of perverse feats in his apartment. However, without realizing it, this step from customer to dealer had taken Mickey into Manhattan's gang-controlled underworld of drugs rife with malevolent criminals who'd kill someone over a quarter. Fortunately, Mickey was such an inept merchant that he wasn't perceived as a major threat, but his goods were sold at such ridiculously low prices that his business was beginning to affect the revenue of one territory, and a slightly annoyed "veterano" had decided to make Mickey's acquaintance.

ᔆ

Across Central Park, another Thanksgiving morning was unfolding. Dr. Bright had planned on spending the day with friends in Albany, but Howard Fontaine had called at eight o'clock in the morning and had begged him to come over because Dawn had returned. The doctor normally didn't make house calls, especially on holidays, but he was concerned about Dawn. Besides, his friends Upstate were a tiresome lot, and this provided the perfect excuse not to go.

Before Dr. Bright pressed the bell, Howard Fontaine, a plump and nervous little man with stray hairs swept over his bald spot, opened the door. He shook the doctor's hand and pulled him into the apartment. After closing the door, Howard walked over to a window and stared outside as if the most tragic scene in the world were taking place out there. Dr. Bright interrupted the silence by clearing his throat, and for a moment Howard looked at him like he'd forgotten who the doctor was. When the light of recognition finally brightened his eyes, Howard said that Dr. Lowenstein, the family psychiatrist, was with Louisa in their bedroom. Then, he indicated his daughter's whereabouts with a wave of his hand, and stared out the window again. When Dr. Bright began to suggest a plan of action, Howard dropped into his chair and spilled forth a waterfall of words. He said that everything was his fault because he'd always spoiled Dawn. He rattled off a litany of examples to support the accusation. Then, without any segue, Howard said it was all Louisa's fault. He said she'd never loved Dawn, and had always made a point of saying hateful things to the girl. When Dr. Bright asked what kinds of hateful things had been said, a few tears dripped from Howard's bloodshot eyes.

"She'd say, 'I hate you' to Dawn and threaten to throw her out the window… then one day, I came home for lunch… the house was completely quiet and that window," Howard pointed to the same window he'd been looking out, "was wide open." He closed his eyes. "That was the scariest moment of my life, Doctor. I really thought I was going to see her tiny little body on the pavement, but then…" He opened his eyes. "I heard sobbing in the bedroom."

"Was it Louisa?"

"Yes. She was curled up in a ball with Dawn beside her… then I …" He attempted to take a deep breath and sort of choked at the same time.

"Then you what?" Dr. Bright said, wanting the pages of the man's story to be turned quicker.

"Well, I wasn't thinking clearly… all sorts of things were running through my mind and… and I rushed to the bed screaming, 'What have you done?!'" His head fell into his hands. "Oh, Doctor, that's the worst thing I've ever done in my life."

Dr. Bright was so caught up in the story that he trembled when Howard referred to him.

"I wish you could've seen them," he said, slowly raising his head. "Louisa's body all limp like she'd been hit by a car and Dawn looking up at me with the most interesting little smile."

"Interesting in what way?" Dr. Bright asked.

"Like she knew."

Even though Howard's reply was cryptic, Dr. Bright knew what he meant. Somewhere in her little spirit, Dawn had sensed victory.

The gold clock ticking on the wall said ten o'clock. Dr. Bright had now been sitting there with Howard for a little over an hour. Then a shrill voice crying "Dad" filled the room, and Howard flew out of his chair. A few moments later, Howard beckoned Dr. Bright from a partially opened door. Then he practically pushed him into a darkened room. It took a moment for Dr. Bright's eyes to adjust to the turbid light as a bedroom slowly emerged, with curtains drawn, clothes all over the floor, and Dawn fully dressed on the unmade bed.

"Say, Dawn, do you think we could open the curtains?" Dr. Bright asked.

"No, I like them closed," she said, and started laughing.

"What's so funny?" he inquired.

"I was just thinking that the only person I'd rather not be is you."

"Meaning?"

"*Meaning,*" she mimicked him, "I'd trade places with anyone but you."

"No, I understand what you mean, but why wouldn't you want to trade places with me?"

"Why?" She pulled open the curtains, "Look at you!" Daylight spilled all over him like cheap yellow paint.

"You're standing in this fucked up kid's room on fucking Thanksgiving morning! You must have no fucking life at all!"

Her words made his throat tight.

"Don't you have any friends? Jesus Christ, Doctor. At least I have a few friends."

"But, Dawn this isn't about my life… "

"Yes, it is! Yes, it fucking is!" she shouted. "You people all say that, but it's bullshit! I'm expected to talk to you? Who the fuck are you? Where do you get off helping people with their lives when yours is so fucked up?"

"I… "

"You're not perfect!" she screamed.

"I never said I was."

"So why don't you go home and work on your miserable life and leave me alone to deal with mine!"

He felt like a silent film cowboy with a hundred arrows sticking in him as she closed the curtain, rolled over, and faced the wall.

When Dr. Bright left Dawn's room, he had expected to find Howard, but the living room was empty, and except for the gold clock ticking on the wall, the apartment was as silent as a tomb. He wanted to leave a note, but because he was already beginning to feel like an intruder, the thought of looking for paper and pen filled him with anxiety, so he just left.

☙

Who the fuck are you? Dawn had asked, and when Dr. Bright got back to his apartment, he tried to answer her complicated question. Looking down at a barren Eighty-sixth Street normally teeming with buses and cabs, the first word that came to his mind was lonely. He and Margot, his wife of twenty years, had gotten divorced last summer, and he still hadn't wrapped his mind around it—there hadn't been any infidelities, money was never an issue, and they had a lovely daughter, Zoe, now an engineering major at Cal Poly. Dr. Bright had thought they had the perfect marriage until Margot, upon returning from a trip to see her parents, informed him that she wanted to move back to Buffalo. At first, he thought she was kidding because she had always referred to her hometown as a "frozen shit hole." Located on the shores of Lake Erie, Buffalo gets pounded by snow in the winter, pummeled by rain in the spring and hammered by suffocating humidity and mosquitoes the rest of the year. However, when she began researching homes in that area, he realized she was serious.

When Dr. Bright expressed his bewilderment, Margot said that her life had been empty since Zoe left, and she wanted to take care of her parents to restore a semblance of meaning. Confusion turned to sorrow as the intimacy he had imagined between them turned out to be an illusion—her decision to move to Buffalo had torn away the veil that had carefully concealed the colossal rift in their marriage. Sensing the end was near, Dr. Bright attempted reconciliation in the form of a candlelit dinner at Tavern on the Green, a fancy restaurant located in the heart of Central Park, and amidst the twinkling lights strewn like fallen stars throughout the branches, Margot laid into him—she called him a self-absorbed narcissist. She said he cared more about his practice than his family. As she rattled off myriad examples of his inattention and disinterest, he suddenly noticed she wasn't wearing her wedding ring, and Margot, perceiving his astonishment, told him that she'd taken it off three months ago. When he looked up there were tears in her eyes, for he had unwittingly pounded the final nail into their coffin.

৩১

When Dr. Bright got to the office the following Monday, there were a few important messages on his machine. Howard Fontaine was wondering if Dawn could come at four. The other was Detective Kelly from the Seventeenth precinct saying Zander had turned himself in for assaulting his mother (even though technically speaking no one had been looking for him). Dr. Bright called Howard and told him four o'clock would be fine. Then, he called the cop.

"Yeah, Doc. We couldn't get in contact with his father, and his mother's in Lenox Hill Hospital, so we're not really sure what to do with him. Maybe we'll keep..."

"You're going to keep him in jail, Detective?" Dr. Bright asked.

"Look, Doc, the kid assaulted his mother. Now, normally we'd send him over to the Juvenile Detention Center, but... "

"Well, doesn't he have any relatives?" the doctor probed.

"Hey, Doc, I got an idea, why don't you take him?"

"Me?" Dr. Bright guffawed at the detective's utterly inappropriate suggestion.

"Yeah. You. You're so concerned and everything. And you're available."

"Well, of course I'm concerned, but I can't take care of him. I mean, I'm his psychologist... and regarding my availability... I work all day and my apartment is..."

"Yeah, yeah, yeah. Well, look Doc, he wants to see ya today."

"He said that?"

"No, he drew me a picture," said the detective facetiously.

"Well," said Doctor Bright, perusing his appointment book, "Does ten-thirty work for you?"

"Sure," the detective responded. "Seventeenth Precinct. Ask for Mark Kelly."

"Okay, but I'm just coming down to talk with him. I'm not promising to take him with me when I leave," Dr. Bright said, and then realized that the detective had already hung up.

∽

Dr. Bright hated Midtown Manhattan, especially Midtown in the morning while trapped inside a cab. When it took twenty minutes to get from Fifty-third Street to Fifty-second Street, he got out early and walked a few blocks with the agitated throng of people. Once inside the Seventeenth Precinct, a cop the size of Long Island stared down at him, picked up a phone, and pointed to a bench. Dr. Bright sat between two interesting characters. There was a woman who smelled like the men's room in Penn Station, and a man dressed up like Madonna circa 1982. Dr. Bright was relieved when Detective Mark Kelly rounded the corner. With his square head, broad shoulders, and jaw of granite, the detective looked like one of those thugs in a Dick Tracy cartoon.

"You Zander's doctor?" the gumshoe asked.

"Yes."

They both thought about shaking hands, but didn't. While waiting for the elevator, the detective struck up a conversation.

"Hey Doc, let me ask you something."

"Of course," the doctor politely replied.

"Well, what the hell's wrong with that kid anyway?"

"What do you mean?" Dr. Bright asked.

"Well, he doesn't seem to be psychotic or anything."

"Zander's not psychotic."

"But he punched his mother in the face!"

"He didn't punch her," Dr. Bright responded. "He slapped her," but once the words were out of his mouth he realized how insignificant the difference was.

Here, the elevator doors opened, and the two men got separated in the melee of people getting on and off. On the fourth floor, they squeezed out. After walking down a hall the color of calamine lotion, they entered a room where Zander was sitting with handcuffs on, watching a small TV.

"Detective, are those necessary?" Dr. Bright said, pointing to the handcuffs.

"No, not at all. He wanted to wear them. Right, Zander?"

"Yeah, man!" Zander displayed them in the air.

"I'll leave you two alone." The detective walked out suppressing a smile.

"So, how's it going, Zander?" Dr. Bright asked the incarcerated teen.

"Fine, man, how's it going with you?!"

"Good, good," said Dr. Bright, stunned to find the boy so happy. "So where did they find you?"

"Find me? Those chumps could never find me. I found them."

"Oh yeah? How did that happen?" the doctor inquired.

"Well, I ran outta money, so I came here and told these faggots who I was."

"Really? What did you say?"

"I said, 'Hey dickheads, I'm the kid who smacked his mom!'"

"And what did they say?" Dr. Bright asked.

"They said, 'Well then, have a seat you evil little bastard and we'll be with ya in a minute!'"

"That's nice, Zander. Listen, your mother's doing fine."

The boy's face darkened. "That's a shame."

"But she's not getting out of the hospital until Wednesday, and your father's not around…"

"Yeah, so what's new?" he said gloomily.

"Anyway, you can't get out of here without a parent or guardian, so…"

"Good, man, I like it here!"

"You like it *here*?" Dr. Bright scanned the grim surroundings.

"Fuck yeah, man! All the creeps and whores. It's fuckin' cool!"

"But Zander…"

"I heard some ho givin' head last night!"

"Okay, okay, but listen Zander, Detective Kelly couldn't find any of your relatives and for some reason he suggested that you stay with me. What do you think?" Dr. Bright could hardly believe he'd uttered the ludicrous offer.

"With you?!" Zander cried in disgust as if he'd just swallowed a worm.

"Yeah, it's only for two nights and besides…"

"Listen, man, seeing you forty-five minutes once a week is too much for me," the boy retorted.

"Well, I work during the day and wouldn't be home until five or six."

"Yeah, and when you got home we'd roast marshmallows and talk about our feelings," Zander said sardonically.

"No. But you'd have a safer place than this to sleep."

"Forget it, man. Besides, how do I know you're not some sort of sick child molester?"

"Zander, give me a break," Dr. Bright protested.

"I'm not saying you *are* a child molester," the teen continued. "I'm saying how can I be sure you're not?"

"I guess you can't be sure. But you can be pretty sure of one thing, Zander."

"What's that?"

"You can be pretty sure that at least one of the creeps in this building has molested a kid."

"Yeah, well, if they come near me, I'll fuckin' kill 'em!" He stood up and shook the handcuffs at Dr. Bright.

"Look, Zander, I'm not some goddamn pedophile. I came down here because I care. Now do you want to stay in this dump or come home with me?"

"I wanna stay here!"

"Fine."

Before going to work, Dr. Bright wanted to drop by and see Sharon at the hospital. Because the streets were still a clamorous knot of cabs, trucks, and buses, he took the subway. While waiting for a train, the doctor perused the graffiti—a yellow king wearing a five-pointed throne dominated the landscape. Dr. Bright knew it was a gang sign, but its origin eluded him. After boarding the train, he realized how long it had been since he'd ridden the subway. Because he spent most of his time in his office which was three blocks away from his home, he rarely left the Upper East Side, and when he did venture out of his neighborhood, he usually took a cab. He made mental notes of the differences since his last subterranean journey, but one characteristic captured his attention— all the commuters were tied to their phones like balloons dependent on fragile strings, and he mused that if their devices suddenly died, they'd probably float to the ceiling then drift away when the doors opened at Seventy-seventh Street. However, his contemplation was pierced by a stab of disappointment because it occurred to him that the world had changed, and he hadn't realized it.

The familiar entanglement of gurneys and wheelchairs at the entrance of Lenox Hill Hospital was strangely comforting to Dr. Bright. After passing through a labyrinth of pale hallways, he located Sharon's room. His hand, poised to knock, was suspended in motion by the sight of her in bed—bathed in sunlight from a window, her face looked radiant, and the contours of her supple body were revealed by her tenuous gown.

"Oh, Doctor, I didn't see you there." Her words were strung together and flat.

"Hi, Sharon. How are you feeling?" Dr. Bright said feeling abashed because she had caught him looking at her.

"Oh, I feel okay." She touched her swollen cheek. "They say I can leave Wednesday."

"That's good."

"Doctor, have you seen Zander?"

"Yes he's…"

"Is he with his father?" she asked with a worried tone.

"No, actually, they couldn't find his father."

"That figures." Her eyes grew dark.

"And I guess you don't have any other relatives here?" Dr. Bright inquired delicately.

"No, not here." She looked at her hands. "So then he's…"

"So I took him."

"You took him?" Her face lit up like a morning sky.

"Yes…"

"Oh, Doctor!" She grabbed her mouth, closed her eyes, then resumed her labored discourse. "See a policeman called here and I thought…"

"Sharon, I'd never leave him there." He lied with the plan of fixing the situation.

Back at the Seventeenth Precinct, after Dr. Bright explained the predicament, he and Detective Kelly collaborated on a lie about a creepy halfway house where

Zander would have to go if he didn't go home with Dr. Bright. At first, their efforts bore no fruit. Zander liked the idea of spending some time with homeless people, drug addicts, and prostitutes. But when Detective Kelly suggested he'd have to share a bed with somebody, the boy popped right up and demanded to be released.

Zander wasn't at all impressed with the doctor's CD collection, and asked who the fuck The Who were. When Dr. Bright explained that they had played at Woodstock, the boy called it "hippie trash." Then, he told the doctor that "the fat whore in the picture" (referring to a Botticelli print) could be his "next bitch" if she lost thirty pounds. But Zander's eyes lit up when he saw the flat-screen plasma TV, and he held the remote in his hand as if it were the Holy Grail.

As Dr. Bright was leaving, he tried giving a few instructions. But Zander was already sailing the insipid seas of high-definition digital television. So, the doctor walked to his office with visions of finding his apartment building burned to the ground when he got home.

℃

His first client today was Stan, the once successful financial advisor until cocaine destroyed his career. His addiction had culminated in a high-speed police pursuit along FDR Drive that ended when his Mercedes hit a guard rail in Battery Park sending the unbuckled teenage prostitute from the backseat into the front seat. Miraculously, no one was seriously hurt, but Stan's life sustained several injuries—he lost his license, he lost his job, and his wife had left him.

One of the conditions of the court was mandatory drug counseling, and Stan had completed the six-month program. However, even though Dr. Bright had encouraged him to continue NA, his client rejected the idea.

"Look, Doctor, I'm clean. I don't need to sit around with a bunch of drug addicts," Stan said bitterly.

Dr. Bright could tell that Stan hadn't come to terms with his addiction because of his disdain for those afflicted by the same thing.

"But Stan, they're wrestling with substance abuse just like you," the doctor challenged him.

"Just like me?!" The man exploded with laughter. "Those bottom-feeding lowlifes? Not a chance!"

Dr. Bright was worried about Stan because the arrogance that first led him down the dark road of drugs was waiting to beguile him again.

❧

When Dawn walked in, Dr. Bright didn't know who it was at first. She had dyed her hair green, or had tried to anyway. Her clothes were different, too. Her style had gone from Upper East Side (known for its wealth) to Alphabet City (a seedy but fashionable section of Manhattan).

"Where was I, right? Isn't that what you were going to ask?" she asked combatively.

"What makes you think I was going to ask that, Dawn?"

"Well, isn't that what my parents are paying you for?"

"Not that I know of."

She spun around in the swivel chair. When it finally came to a stop, her eyes rested on him and she smiled.

"So, any more issues at home, Dawn?"

"Not really." Her smile faded. "Fatso's been taking her Xanax, so things have been pretty calm."

"Oh?" the doctor inquired.

"Bitch takes Xanax, Valium, Lithium, Zoloft. Dr. Lowenstein's orders."

"Lowenstein?" He scanned his memory. "He was there on Thanksgiving, right?"

"Oh!" She exploded in laughter. "You met him?" She stood up, stuck out her hand, and said in a humid voice, "Name's Lowenstein."

Dr. Bright shook her little hand. "Nice to finally meet you, Dr. Lowenstein."

"So, what's your diagnosis of Dawn?" the girl said, still imitating her mother's psychiatrist.

"Well…" he started laughing at her posture and the double chin she was making.

"Out with it, man! What's wrong with the little bitch?" Dawn asked.

"Well, Dr. Lowenstein, I'd say Dawn was suffering from an acute case of adolescence."

"Cut the technical crap! Give it to me straight!"

"Okay," Dr. Bright continued, "I'd say she's a smart, sensitive kid doing her best to cope with a challenging home life."

"Talk to me about the home life." She snatched a piece of paper and pencil off his desk, and started to write things down.

"Well, Dawn seems to have a pretty good relationship with her father, but her mother…"

"Yes." She stopped writing and looked at him. "What about the mother?"

"Well, they don't get along."

"Must be the little bitch's fault." She started writing again.

"Well, I don't think it's anyone's fault…"

"Ah, you talking shrinks are all the same." She crumpled up the paper and threw it into the trash can.

And even though her dig wasn't aimed at him, Dr. Bright somehow felt like she'd thrown him into the trash can.

"I say medicate the little bastards. Get 'em to shut up. Problem is all the talk."

"Dawn, have you heard him say…"

"Name's Lowenstein!" She cut him off.

"Come on, Dawn."

"Okay, okay." She sat back down in the swivel chair.

"Does Dr. Lowenstein say things like that?"

"Oh, hell yeah. He thinks they should have me put away."

"You've heard him say that?" Dr. Bright asked.

"He's been saying it for years! If I stand in my closet, I can hear everything they say. That's how I found out I was adopted." As she stared off with ceramic eyes, his heart broke for the little girl standing in her closet that day.

4

Because there wasn't any smoke coming from his apartment building that evening, Dr. Bright felt slightly relieved. In fact, when he walked in, Zander was just sitting there watching TV with a kid dressed in black. L Train, as Zander called him, was wearing a t-shirt advertising a rock band called "Cerebral Hemorrhage." An appropriate name, thought the doctor, for it seemed quite possible that L Train had a few rips in the lining of his cerebral cortex.

Dr. Bright instantly noticed the two forty-ounce Budweisers poorly concealed beneath his glass coffee table.

"Don't you guys want glasses for those?" he said, pointing at the badly hidden booze.

The boys looked at each other in astonishment. Then Zander replied sheepishly, "Nah, man, we like 'em like this."

"Well, at least put them on the table. I don't want them to spill," Dr. Bright suggested.

They looked at each other again, slowly took their beers off the floor, and placed them on the table.

"You guys hungry?" Dr. Bright asked.

"Nah, man, not me," said Zander, looking at the TV.

"How about you, L Train?"

L Train looked up at Dr. Bright with abject bewilderment, swallowed, then pointed at Zander.

"Okay, well, if you guys were hungry and I was ordering food, what kind of food would you want?"

The boys looked at each other then back at the TV.

So Dr. Bright ordered two large pizzas, because that's what he had liked when he was young. And he couldn't believe how much they ate. L Train probably weighed 140 pounds tops with his combat boots and Gothic spiked jewelry on. Yet he devoured a large pizza, except for the slice Dr. Bright had rescued for himself, in less than half an hour. Zander, who looked like a wafer-thin refugee, ate half of the other pizza, which was piled to the ceiling with pepperoni, black olives, and mushrooms. Dr. Bright put a moratorium on the beer, which was met with little resistance. However, the boys did drink all the milk the doctor had for his morning cereal.

At eleven o'clock, Dr. Bright asked L Train where he lived, hoping he'd leave. But Zander said that L Train's mother had kicked him out three weeks ago, and that he didn't live anywhere. Unable to hit that ball back over the net, Dr. Bright told L Train he could stay if he didn't mind sharing the pullout sofabed with Zander. The boys looked at each other like someone in the room had just farted. Then Zander made it abundantly clear that he'd rather have needles shoved into his eyes than share a bed with L Train. And L Train intimated with a series of grunts and gesticulations that the floor would be fine. The fact that Dr. Bright was beginning to understand L Train alarmed him to a degree.

Around four a.m., Dr. Bright saw the blue light of the television playing beneath his door. He figured the boys were out there watching porn. But he found Zander snoring on the couch, and L Train sitting up straight with closed eyes like a dead person the cops hadn't found yet. So, the doctor tiptoed through the pile of teenage carnage, found the remote, and turned off the TV.

The next morning Dr. Bright decided it would be really stupid to leave L Train and Zander alone in his apartment all day. So he woke up L Train with the plan of putting him in a cab. Outside in the bright morning light, with his greasy hair, black fingernails, and funereal complexion, L Train looked even scarier. And it wasn't until the eleventh empty cab passed them that Dr. Bright realized why they weren't stopping. Therefore, he asked L Train to buy a paper while he hailed down the cab. Just as L Train was coming back from the kiosk, a cab pulled up. Upon seeing the funky cargo Dr. Bright deposited into his car, the driver looked alarmed. But L Train's request to go just a few blocks away seemed to appease the hack a bit.

Zander was still sleeping when Dr. Bright came back. His apartment now looked like a college dorm room with the fully-dressed kid on the couch, the forty-ounce Budweisers on the table, and two pizza boxes on the floor. One of the boxes was smashed in. The other had its top flipped open like a broken-down car by the side of the road. The doctor quietly took the two pizza boxes and put them in a big garbage bag. Upon finding a piece of pepperoni near Zander's discarded shoe, he began combing the floor on his hands and knees. People shouldn't leave food out in New York City, he thought, because battalions of scary roaches are always on the hunt. And some of those bugs are scary—they're big, they have antennae, dark red wings, and bad attitudes. Aside from a notorious band of crumbs, the doctor's search uncovered three olives commiserating beneath the couch and two mushrooms by the wall.

"I knew you were a fuckin' child molester," Zander said with a raspy voice.

"Good morning, Zander," Dr. Bright said, crouched on all fours beside the couch.

"What the fuck are you doin', Doc?"

"I'm trying to get this place cleaned up," the doctor answered.

"Where's L Train?"

"He left," the doctor said, shoving the mushrooms and olives into the garbage bag.

"When did he leave?" Zander sat up and checked his pockets.

"About fifteen minutes ago."

"That fuckin' prick!" Zander shouted.

"What's the matter, Zander?"

"Nothin'."

"Are you sure?"

"Yeah," he stared at L Train's chair. "He's got somethin' a mine, that's all."

"Can you call him?"

"Nah." He got up and looked around. "I don't got his number."

"We can look it up in the phone book," Dr. Bright suggested.

"Nah, I don't know where he lives."

"Well, Zander, I think he said he was going to Seventy-ninth and Fifth."

"L Train? He don't fuckin' live on Seventy-ninth and Fifth."

"Well, that's where he was going."

The light of recognition filled the boy's eyes. "That fuckin' prick!"

"What's the matter, Zander?"

"He's goin' to the fuckin' park!" the teen exclaimed.

"What's wrong with that?"

Zander grabbed his coat and headed for the door.

"Wait a second, Zander…"

"What?" He opened the door.

"I was going to have a key made so you could get back in."

"I don't need a key, Doc."

"But how will you…"

"I'll stop by your office!" he said, running down the stairs and out of the building towards Central Park.

∽

Morning felt like it was already evening, but Dr. Bright still had a full day ahead of him. After some early appointments, he had Brenda Fixx at two o'clock. With a pile of dyed blonde hair sitting above her weathered face, penciled-in eyebrows, and artificially impregnated lips, Brenda was a cosmetic car accident. She was the proprietor of a small business in Chelsea who firmly believed that there were two working brains in the world: she owned one, while everybody else shared the other. His three o'clock was Evelyn, the attorney who invented men. And his last appointment was Dawn.

Brenda either had a cocaine addiction or a chronic sinus infection, because every two minutes or so she snorted loudly. And as many times as she'd done it, Dr. Bright still got scared when it happened. For it sounded like that suck the kitchen sink makes after the Liquid Plumber has eaten through all the food clogging its throat.

"And your employees still come to work late?" Dr. Bright asked.

"Oh they come late, they call in sick, and they wear sweaters…"

"I'm sorry, Brenda, did you say they wear sweaters?"

"Yes!" she snorted.

"They're not supposed to wear sweaters?"

"It's a sunglasses store!" she shouted at him.

"I'm sorry, Brenda, I…"

"A sunglasses store," she said, smiling like he was a moron. "You know those dark glasses people wear to keep the sun out?"

"Yes, Brenda, I know what sunglasses are, but I don't see why…"

"Because sunglasses are for summer. You know sun, summer…" She tilted her head and snorted again.

"Oh, I see, and sweaters…"

"Exactly," she clapped her hands. "Sweaters are for winter."

A bright rose of satisfaction painted Brenda's cheek as Dr. Bright tried to figure out what they had just talked about. After assembling the scattered conversation, he suggested she turn up the heat for her employees, and she explained that turning up the heat was a stupid idea because she'd have to pay a higher electric bill. Then, she told him to butt out, which made him consider his clients' various motivations for coming. There were those who came because they truly wanted to get better. There were those forced into counseling by their parents, like Zander and Dawn. Then, there were those, like Brenda Fixx, who came to argue. Whenever Dr. Bright asked a question, she'd ask him a question about his question. And whenever he offered suggestions, like today, she'd tell him how stupid his ideas were. Then she'd tell him to butt out, citing his inexperience in all matters.

But the thing Dr. Bright looked forward to most was Brenda's monthly scrutiny of his bill. Two years ago, he had raised his rates without telling her (an oversight on his part) and the following Tuesday she had burst into his office with the bill clenched in her fist. For ten excruciating minutes words like "embezzler," "thief," "fraud," and "extortionist" had rained down on him. He was eventually able to get her to begrudgingly accept his apology. But the incident inflamed an already smoldering sense of distrust. Now, she brought in the bill at the beginning of every month, even though it hadn't changed in two years.

With ten minutes left in the session, Brenda looked at her watch and asked if they were done for the day.

"We can be," said Dr. Bright.

She started snorting as she rummaged through her purse.

"Brenda?"

"What?" She didn't look up.

"Are you sure you don't want to talk about anything else?" Dr. Bright asked.

"Oh fuck! Mother fuck!" she yelled.

"What is it, Brenda?"

"I forgot my fucking keys!"

"Are you sure?"

"Here!" She violently spilled the contents of her purse all over his desk. "See for yourself!"

He looked at the rolling lipsticks, crumpled receipts, compacts, pens, tampons, tissues, wallet, bottles of different pills, and finally at the shaking hand sweeping them back together.

"I suppose you think I'm stupid!" she roared.

"I don't think you're stupid, Bren…"

"Two hundred dollars to have you tell me I didn't lose my keys!"

"I'm…"

"When I did lose my keys!" She brushed the pile back into her purse, which was open between her thighs. "Is this what you do all day, *doctor*?" Her sardonic emphasis on "doctor" sparked a realization in his mind. Psychology is a respected field, and in New York City, psychologists are deemed as necessary as plumbers. However, the butterflies of skepticism still abound because psychology deals with the incorporeal landscape of emotions, whereas a plumber fixes *things*, and even has a box of tools.

"Christ, I thought I had an easy job, but you!" She stood up and snorted. "You've got the job of a lifetime! I mean two hundred dollars an hour to… to… I wish I thought of that!"

"Yes, well, we're out of time for today, Brenda, but next week we can…"

She walked out the door snorting.

Dr. Bright had arranged it so that Evelyn's appointment would follow Brenda's, because after forty-five minutes of tedious arguing, it was nice to be productive again. Not to say those minutes with Brenda were a total waste; she did get to leave some of her frustrations in his office. And if it weren't for their weekly sessions, she'd probably excoriate her employees even more. So, by submitting to her weekly invectives, he felt he was helping out some poor soul.

⌘

"Oh now, Doctor, I don't want to talk about my anxiety today," Evelyn said while looking into a compact mirror.

"Why not, Evelyn?"

"Because I'm in a good mood for a change. Remember Peter, the doctor? Well, he's asked me to marry him."

"That's wonderful, Evelyn. Congratulations," Dr. Bright said, trying to muster a jolly tone.

"You don't sound too pleased, Doctor. You're thinking about his mother, aren't you?"

"I…" he began.

"Well, don't worry, because the most wonderful thing has happened!" She cut him off.

"Really, what?"

"She died!" Evelyn smiled into her mirror once more then put it in her purse. "I know that sounds awful, but she was sick anyway, and all she ever did was bother us. So why shouldn't I be happy?"

"I understand, Evelyn."

"No, you don't. I can see it in your eyes. You think I'm a horrible bitch, don't you?" Her tone instantly darkened.

"Evelyn, I don't think anything of the…"

"Bullshit!" She pounded on her knees with her hands, then covered her face with them. "I'm sorry, Doctor," she said, trying to wipe the mascara off her cheeks, but smearing it in the process. "It's not you… it's… I know Peter loves me, but sometimes…"

"Sometimes what?" he asked.

"Well, sometimes I feel like he's marrying me for the wrong reasons. I mean, he suddenly gets serious when his mother gets sick… so I wonder if he's not just using me… but if I'm not there for him now, what does that say about me?"

"Well, do you have to marry every guy whose mother dies?" he asked.

"No, but…"

"I just don't think his mother's death should have any bearing on whether you marry him or not, Evelyn," Dr. Bright said, remembering that Peter, like the rest of her lovers, was spun from the loom of her imagination.

"But Doctor… that sounds so cold," her voice trembled.

"Why?"

"Because his mother just died."

"Look, Evelyn, it's sad that his mother just died, but I don't think you should marry him out of pity."

At the mention of the word "pity," her eyes grew dark and she went off on a tangent about the difference between loyalty and pity. Then, her discourse ceased and her eyes welled up with tears again. Dr. Bright was tempted to say something but he chose to honor her long-suppressed pain with silence. After a few moments, she withdrew a tissue from her purse, wiped her eyes and stood up.

"Lately I always leave here feeling worse," she said, walking out.

Dr. Bright began typing a summary of the session with Evelyn at his computer by the window. However, he kept getting distracted by the streaks of dying sunlight on the brownstone next door, and it occurred to him that he was exhausted. Because Evelyn had departed fifteen-minutes early he had some time before Dawn's appointment, so he closed his eyes, and instantly fell into a deep sleep until a shrill "*Cock A Doodle Do!!!*" awoke him.

Spinning around, his eyes popping open, Dr. Bright saw Dawn. "What... what time is it?" he asked.

"Four-thirty," she said, holding her stomach, still snickering.

"You're a half hour late, Dawn."

"My, aren't we touchy today," she said, flopping down in the swivel chair.

"No, I just..." He stopped himself.

"Do you wanna tell me about it, Doctor?" she asked curiously.

"There's really nothing to tell."

"See, here's what I don't get. You expect me to trust you, but you don't trust me."

"It's not that I don't trust you, Dawn..."

She glared at him with porcelain eyes.

"Well, if you really must know, I'm a little tired because I had two unexpected guests last night. But I'm here to help you so…"

"How do you know you're not helping me?" she asked. "See, I think I'd trust you more if things were more…"

"Reciprocal?" He finished her sentence.

"What does that mean, doctor?"

"More mutual, more equal?"

"Yeah, more equal. See, you guys expect us to tell you things we don't even tell our best friends, but we don't even know you."

"Okay, Dawn," he acquiesced. "What do you want to know?"

"What happened last night?"

"Last night… oh, right, last night. One of my clients didn't have a place to stay, so I let him stay with me."

"He didn't have a place to stay, so you just brought him home?" Dawn inquired with an incredulous look on her face.

"Not exactly. See, his mother's in the hospital and his father's not around so…"

"Why is his mother in the hospital?" she probed.

"She has a broken jaw."

"Cool! Who broke her jaw?"

"Well," he paused and then said, "my client did."

"He broke his mother's fucking jaw! Cool!" She jumped out of her chair.

"And it was either my place or the police station."

"Wow, that is so fucking cool!"

"It wasn't so cool for his mother," Dr. Bright suggested.

"Why not?" She frowned at him.

"Well, aside from being badly injured, she was worried about her son. Anyway, when I realized he'd have to stay in one of those halfway houses, I brought him home."

"When did all of this happen, Doctor?" Dawn sat back down.

"Yesterday."

"Well, that explains it then," Dawn said with smug satisfaction.

"That explains what?"

She started to look through her backpack.

"Dawn?"

"Well, you weren't exactly a barrel of laughs yesterday," she explained.

"Really? I thought our session went very well."

"*You* thought so," she emphasized the pronoun to show him that his perception was skewed.

"Oh… well, look Dawn, if there's ever a time where…"

"And another thing, Doctor." The hard voice didn't match her fragile eyes. "When our sessions are over, don't give me that 'let's pick up here next time' crap. 'Cause no one ever remembers and it's just a line anyway."

"A line?" he asked.

"Yeah, it's just a line to get rid of me." Her fragile blue eyes were about to break.

"It's not to get rid of you, Dawn."

She blinked and a tear appeared.

"And you might not think I remember where we leave off, but I do. For instance, during our last session you were telling me how you found out you were adopted. Remember?"

She stood up and put on her backpack.

"Where are you going, Dawn?"

"It's four-forty-five."

"Well, look, I don't have another client today, so…"

"You think I'm gonna stay here longer than I have to?"

"Well, I just thought…"

"Get real, man!" She walked out the door.

5

When Dr. Bright got home that night he reflected on his day. It had been a bad one. Brenda had yelled at him. Evelyn had left in tears. Dawn had told him to "get real," and there was something about the girl's words that hurt him. She had basically called him a fool, and he wondered if she was right. Yesterday's subway experience flooded his mind—the yellow king on the wall, the commuters consumed by their phones were all part of a world he didn't understand. But, it was the phones, not the gang sign, that had troubled him most because technology represented the most enigmatic part of this new mysterious planet—people were now shopping, voting, and dating online, and a new language had emerged. Esoteric terms like trolling, hashtag, photobomb, and tweet had fallen from his clients' lips, and he was just now owning the fact that he hadn't known what they'd meant. However, his disillusionment led to painful feelings of regret because he realized that this was all related to the self-centeredness that had driven Margot away. Unfortunately, his introspection was cut short by a knocking at his door.

Zander's clothes were torn and muddy, and to say he smelled like liquor would be a gross understatement. He smelled as if Roman soldiers had nearly drowned him in cheap wine and then spent an afternoon kicking him around the Coliseum.

"Hey, Doc!" his drunken client yelled.

"Leave those in the hall, please," said Dr. Bright, pointing to Zander's muddy boots.

"What? Leave what?"

"Your boots."

"Aw, c'mon Doc." Zander started to come in.

"No." Dr. Bright pushed him back. "Leave them in the hall."

"Fine," Zander started tugging at the laces, then fell down laughing.

"Jesus." Dr. Bright bent down and untied the murky strings.

"Hey, Doc! You're better at that than my mom!"

"Don't get used to it," the doctor cautioned him.

Zander reluctantly kicked off his shoes and they both walked into the apartment.

"Are you hungry, Zander?"

"Don't got any beer, do ya, Doc?" The boy smiled with all his teeth, like a monkey.

"No."

"Any whiskey, vodka, rum?"

"No, Zander. I don't drink."

"Not even a fuckin' glass of wine with dinner? Nice cold beer at a baseball game?"

"Nope," the doctor responded.

"Do ya ever go to baseball games, Doc?"

"Sure."

"Well, whaddya drink when you're there?" Zander inquired.

"Diet soda or…"

"DIET SODA! Diet Soda's fuckin' gross, Doc!"

"Fine. So, Zander…"

"It tastes like fuckin' horse piss!" He fell back onto the couch. "At least get yourself a real fuckin' soda!"

"I will, Zander."

"They have them big ass cups a' Coke there," he said, showing the dimensions with his hands. "Me an' L Train spike 'em with vodka when those pricks won't sell us beer."

"That's nice, Zander," the doctor said sarcastically.

"Big pricks can't stop us." The lids of his eyes began to close. "So… Doc… why don't cha drink?"

"No big reason."

"Were ya a big fuckin' lush or somethin'?"

"No, Zander. It's just a preference."

"Yeah, right," he said, feeling beneath the couch with his hand.

"Can I help you find something, Zander?"

"Where's that fuckin' remote?"

"Oh, I don't know." Dr. Bright looked around. "I always lose it."

"Probly zymbolic huh, Doc?" The boy's words had begun to slur.

"Probably."

Dr. Bright searched for the remote in the usual spots. Beneath his chair, on top of the fridge, next to the lamp. And sure enough, there it was, on top of the microwave behind the box of cereal.

Zander had passed out while he was in the kitchen. And it was at that moment, while gazing down at the boy, that the reality of Zander's life had finally hit Dr.

Bright. Fifteen years old, and he was running around in Central Park with drug addicts, dealers, and perverts. The doctor remembered all of the respected people in his field who had written magazine articles on the state of today's youth. How kids' aggression was all linked to the violent culture they were immersed in (TV, movies, song lyrics, etc.). How their schools were overcrowded, and their teachers didn't care. But as Dr. Bright looked down at this stoned and drunk fifteen-year-old who had passed out on his couch, he didn't see any overcrowded classrooms or apathetic teachers. He saw a kid who had to sleep on his therapist's couch because his father wasn't around.

∾

Morning broke like glass against the apartment buildings. Dr. Bright quietly made a cup of coffee, and while Zander lay snoring on the couch, he looked out the window and began preparing himself for an interesting day—Sharon was getting out of the hospital, and the doctor thought it would be good if he met her there with Zander. He harbored some apprehensions, because Zander hadn't seen her since the incident in his office, and Dr. Bright wasn't sure how the boy would feel. But he decided to go forward with his plan and held a cup of coffee beneath the sleeping boy's nose.

"What the fuck are you doin', man?" Zander asked in a lifeless voice.

"Waking you up," the doctor replied.

The teen looked at the cup, pointed at the table, then closed his eyes.

"Come on, Zander." Dr. Bright waved it under his nose again. "We've got a few things to do this morning."

"Jesus." The boy grabbed the cup with one hand and held his head with the other.

"Want some Advil, Zander?"

"Yeah, man." He sounded like a zombie.

Dr. Bright brought him two Advil tablets and a bottle of Poland Spring water that Zander chugged down in a few furious gulps.

"Got any more a' these, Doc?" he asked, shaking the empty bottle at him.

"Sure. Zander, do you want some breakfast?"

The boy threw a dark look at Dr. Bright.

"Sorry. Wait until the Advil kicks in."

"Waitin'," Zander groaned.

The doctor decided to let Zander recover a bit before broaching the subject of Sharon. And while tidying up the kitchen, he played around with several different openings in his mind—*Zander, your mother's getting out of the hospital today.* No need to remind him she's in the hospital. *Zander, I think we should...* Should is no good. Never tell a kid (or anyone) what they should do. *Zander...* He couldn't decide.

"Zander, we're picking up your mother at ten," Dr. Bright finally blurted out.

"Okay," the boy agreed.

"Are you hungry yet?"

"Nah."

"How about some more coffee?" the doctor asked.

Zander pointed to the cold cup he hadn't touched.

Outside the sunlight leaned against the buildings. Dr. Bright wanted to hail a cab, but Zander wanted to walk, to prolong getting there, most likely. Since Lenox Hill was only a couple blocks away, the doctor agreed to the boy's plan. Third Avenue must have seemed like a nightmare to Zander, the pedestrians moving faster than the cars inching their way through the morning traffic. The doctor felt Zander's relief when they caught the red light at Seventy-ninth. But taking that horrible right onto Seventy-seventh, Dr. Bright sensed the boy's anxiety so he stopped a few times to point out interesting landmarks. Zander pretended to listen with his eyes stuck like gum to the ground. Then they'd move on, slower and slower each time.

Dr. Bright got halfway across Lexington Avenue before he realized Zander wasn't with him. Turning around, he saw the boy on the corner, his hands plunged into his pockets, his face the color of chalk.

"Yo, Doc, I can't do this," Zander said when Dr. Bright returned to the curb.

"Are you sure, Zander?"

"Yeah," he said, looking down.

Dr. Bright was at a loss for words. On the one hand, he thought Zander should go, but on the other hand, he totally understood the boy's position. Yet, more importantly, this was the first time Zander had ever revealed a vulnerable side, and Dr. Bright didn't want to greet the important moment with judgment or contempt.

"I'll tell you what, Zander.... See that diner over there?"

"Yeah," said the boy, still looking down.

"Here," Dr. Bright handed him ten dollars. "Go over there and get some coffee or something to eat. If, after a few minutes, you really want to leave, then leave. But if you decide to come, then come. Deal?"

Zander looked up with pitch black eyes. "Deal."

❧

The swelling in Sharon's face had significantly decreased. In fact, she looked lovely with the rouge of rest on her cheeks. But the color quickly evaporated when she saw that Dr. Bright had come alone.

"Zander's not with you?" Her speech was still slightly affected by the injury.

"No, he's…"

"Oh, that's all right." She waved her feelings away like flies. "I'm just waiting for my release forms. Then I have to ride out in that," she said, pointing to a wheelchair.

"Yes, that's how they do it, Sharon."

"But it was my jaw, not my leg." She knew the wheelchair ride was standard procedure, but she wanted to talk about something.

"Yeah, I know, it's pretty stupid." Dr. Bright went along with the specious script.

"So he stayed with you both nights?" Sharon asked.

"He?"

Her eyes grew stormy. "Zander."

"Oh yes… Zander… I'm sorry. Yes, Zander stayed with me."

"Son of a bitch," she said, glaring at a chart on the wall.

"What's the matter, Sharon?"

"Zander's father didn't call you?"

"No."

"Son of a bitch." The color came back to her cheeks.

"Well," the doctor began, "maybe he'll call when he gets back in town…"

"He's not out of town! And I left your number on his answering machine two days ago!"

"Oh, so he knows that Zander…"

"He knows everything! He just doesn't care!" she cried.

An old nurse came in at the end of Sharon's sentence, spun around, and went back out.

"I'm awfully sorry, Sharon."

"You?" She looked at him, "Why should you be sorry? You've been more of a father to Zander over these last few days than his own father ever was. Oh my God!" She covered her face with her pale hands.

"What is it?" Dr. Bright asked.

"I haven't thanked you yet for letting Zander stay with you!"

"Oh, that's all right, Sharon."

"No, it's not all right, and as soon as everything settles down, we're taking you out for dinner."

The same nurse who'd come in before returned and, perhaps sensing the more tranquil mood, staged her thwarted scene. "You're all set to go, dear. If you'll just sign here." She handed Sharon her release form, then turned her faded eyes on Dr. Bright. "And how are you today, sir?"

"I'm fine, thanks. You?"

"Fine, fine," the nurse said, turning back to Sharon. "Is this your husband?"

"No, no." Sharon smiled. "This is my son's psychologist."

"Oh… yes… well." Her old face flooded with color. "Are you ready to go, dear?"

"Yes, very ready."

Rolling Sharon down the hall, the nurse kept stealing glances at Dr. Bright. But the second their eyes would meet, she'd quickly look away. He thought he saw contempt etched into her old face and speculations tumbled around in his mind. Maybe the nurse had heard what had happened to Sharon and thought it was the doctor's fault. Or maybe she was one of those old-fashioned healers who thought psychology was a crock of shit. But his theories came to a halt when they rounded a corner and found Zander sitting with his eyes closed in an abandoned wheelchair.

"Zander!" Sharon screamed.

Awakened by his mother's voice, Zander rose, walked towards the group, and threw his arms around her neck.

6

Mickey sat by the window in a bar on Amsterdam looking out at the Christmas decorations brightening the cloudy afternoon. Although he had lived here his entire life, he had never seen the city workers hoisting up the giant wreaths or wrapping garland around the electric poles, and there was something magical about their sudden appearance. When he was a boy, his mother had told him that it had been the work of elves, and he remembered her elaborate tales about sleighs filled with tiny tools and one grumpy elf named Frankie who always hit his thumb with a hammer.

Mickey's memories were shattered by the arrival of a Hispanic man holding two shot glasses between his fingers.

"Buena noches," he said, sitting down, handing one of the drinks to Mickey.

There was something nondescript about the unexpected guest—his face and hands were weathered, but he dressed like a teenager. He might have been fifteen or fifty.

"Salute," the man said, raising his glass in the air.

Without taking a sip, Mickey put the shot on the table. "Can I help you with something?"

The man looked at the untouched drink and the light in his eyes flickered. He set his own drink down and pushed it away with his index finger.

"You see, I'm waiting for someone," said Mickey, acknowledging his visitor's disappointment.

"You mean Tiny?" his guest asked.

"Yes!" Mickey replied in amazement. "How did you know I was waiting for Tiny?"

"Tiny ain't coming," the man replied ominously.

"How do you know he isn't coming?"

"Hey, look at that!" The man pointed to a thin ray of sunshine that had crept across their table. "Ain't that beautiful?"

"Yeah… it's…"

"And look, dude!" He pointed to their drinks now incandescent and shouted, "That's a sign!" He picked up their drinks and handed one to Mickey, "Salute!" And this time Mickey drank, hoping it would make him go away.

"Good job," the man said, slapping Mickey on the back and signaling the bartender who immediately brought two more shots and left. "Now let's talk business, muchacho," he stared at Mickey. "Tiny's all done. Now, you're working with me. Understand?"

"Where is Tiny?" Mickey inquired.

"Tiny ain't none of your business, muchacho," the man said fiercely. "Comprende?"

In the past, Mickey would have crumbled beneath intimidation like this, but these past few months had filled him with a precious valor that he wasn't willing to relinquish so quickly.

"Si entiendo," said Mickey, looking at his watch and standing up.

"Hey, where you going, muchacho? We ain't finished yet," the Hispanic man growled.

"Yeah, we are finished, *muchacho*," Mickey replied defiantly.

For a moment, the man looked puzzled. Then, his eyes welled with tears and he began to laugh. "You're making a big mistake, my friend."

"No," said Mickey. "You are."

After leaving the bar, Mickey called and texted Tiny but to no avail. Finally, with mounting anxiety, he went to his dealer's apartment, and though Mickey could hear a dog barking inside, Tiny never answered the door.

The next day, Mickey found out that the man he'd been talking to was named Angel, a lieutenant in the Latin Kings. He also learned that everything between Columbus and Riverside above Fifty-ninth Street was Latin Kings' territory and that all commerce was controlled by them. Although Mickey had acquired some courage recently, he wasn't stupid, and the thought of gang-bangers packing pistols scared him to death. So, he decided to lay low for a while and sell off his remaining goods to wayward teens and junkies in Central Park.

❦

Mickey had so many people coming and going from his apartment that the neighbors began to complain. So, to decrease the flow of traffic, he bought a bike and began delivering his wares. Furthermore, while he enjoyed the pack of stray girls who followed him home every night, he decided to streamline his brood when he realized they were stealing from him. Ironically, it wasn't the small amounts of pilfered cash and drugs that troubled him—he considered those gratuities. Rather, it was the missing silver cigarette case with the 82nd Airborne engraving that had sent him into a rage. The keepsake had belonged to his father, a survivor of dozens of expeditions behind enemy lines in Vietnam who tragically died in a car crash three weeks after returning home. Mickey had never met the man, so the cigarette case was his only palpable connection to him, and he always kept it in the top drawer of his nightstand. Then, one morning while looking for rolling papers, he noticed it was missing.

After turning his apartment upside down, he realized that one of his *little darlings* had snatched it and he conducted a thorough investigation. First, he checked all of the neighborhood pawn shops, figuring the culprit had swapped it for cash, but when his search bore no fruit, he decided to question his girls. One by one, he invited them over for lengthy interrogations using tactics he had read about in books—he got a few stoned to increase their suggestibility, he yelled at a few, and he even blasted the air conditioning to create white noise. But the end result was crying girls in a cold apartment, so he abandoned those strategies. One time, he slapped a girl, but she reduced him to a crumpled heap on the floor by pulling his hair, clawing his eyes and kneeing him in the balls. Therefore, he severed relations with all his strays, changed the locks on his doors, and, to satisfy his carnal desires, began using the escort service owned and operated by his long-time friend and dealer, Tiny Lopez.

Tiny was anything but tiny. He stood six feet, four inches tall and weighed well over four hundred pounds. Mickey remembered the ridicule his friend had faced in elementary school because of his size, and to make matters worse, Tiny's pants hung below his belly, so that the crack of his ass had become part of the natural landscape. Furthermore, his fleshy fissure became a treasure trove of material for the sadistic schoolyard imps—names like "Crackula" and "Thunderpants" followed him on the bus, during recess, and in the halls. However, he endured the worst tortures at lunch where bullies tipped over his tray or threw food at him. They even blew spitballs through straws at his backside to see if they could lodge one in his aperture.

The torture continued through junior high and then in high school, due to a series of serendipitous events, it stopped. Because of his spacey demeanor and the failing grades that had dogged him for years, Tiny had been diagnosed with ADHD and prescribed Ritalin. However, because the condition had been untreated for so long, Tiny's self-esteem had already been crushed, and he wasn't interested in medicine that was going to help him in school, the place he hated most. But when someone offered him five dollars for one of the little orange pills in the locker room one day, he saw a golden opportunity and his ticket out of hell—using the cash he made from his Ritalin sales, he bought pot from a neighbor, sold it to his classmates in the parking lot at lunch, and cleared a thousand dollars in a month. With the money he earned, he bought pants that fit, several pairs of Air Jordans, a Rolex watch, and the transformation from playground chump to Homie G was complete. However, it didn't take long for school officials to notice Tiny's felonious activities and he was expelled for pedaling narcotics on school property. But Tiny and Mickey had remained friends, and now that Mickey needed a trustworthy connection for his burgeoning business and girls who wouldn't steal, he contacted his big buddy.

7

Dr. Bright contracted salmonella eating tainted chicken at a Christmas party and spent the holiday throwing up. His return to work after a week of dysentery would have been refreshing if Brenda Fixx hadn't been his first client.

"Let me get this straight, Brenda. You want this session to be free because I cancelled our appointment last week and didn't give you twenty-four hours' notice?"

"Yes," she snorted.

"But I called you the night before," he explained.

"Yes, but our appointment was for two and you called me at seven and that's not twenty-four hours." She snorted again.

"Brenda, are you angry with me?" he asked.

"Don't try to change the subject, Doctor!" She snorted a snort that startled him.

"I'm not trying to change the…"

"Yes you are! Yes you are!" she screamed.

"Okay, okay take it easy…" he said softly.

"Don't tell me to take it easy, and don't tell me I'm angry!" She almost got out of her chair.

"Okay, you're not angry."

"And don't tell me I'm not angry!"

"Okay." He fingered a pile of unopened mail. "I won't tell you anything."

"Now, do I have to pay for the session or not?"

"You don't *have* to do anything, Brenda."

"Oh, don't give me that bullshit," she said, sniffing.

"What bullshit?"

"*You don't have to do anything, Brenda*," she said, waving her hands in an unflattering parody of him.

"But you don't," he assured her.

"Oh sure, and then you'll sue me…"

"Brenda, what the hell are you talking about?"

The word hell made her eyes pop open and he remembered that she was a Catholic. His mother had been the same way. Duncan could say "shit," "prick," "asshole," and "bitch." He could use "fuck" in all of its various forms, from "motherfucker" to "fuck you." But if he had said "hell" or made any disparaging reference to God, she'd drag him to confession by his hair.

"So, then I don't have to pay for the two sessions?" Brenda asked.

"No." He started to laugh.

"What are you laughing at?"

"Come on, Brenda. You're trying to pick a fight with me."

"I'm not trying to pick a fight with you. I just want what's mine!"

Dr. Bright suppressed a smile, "You mean you want today's session for free because I cancelled last week? I thought we already decided that."

"But that's not your policy!" she exploded.

"Well, now it is my policy and now it's your policy, too."

"What do you mean?" she snorted.

"If I don't give you twenty-four hours' notice, you don't have to pay."

She mouthed his words to make sure she wasn't being tricked and then said, "That's right."

"Good. I'm glad that's settled."

She frowned at her watch and snorted.

"So, Brenda, how's work going?" he asked with the hope of starting a new conversation.

"Oh… I don't know," she said, still frowning at her watch.

"Isn't it working?" he inquired.

"Huh?" she looked up and snorted.

"I said is there something wrong with it?" Dr. Bright pointed to his own watch.

"No, it's working fine, but I just realized something. We just spent half an hour talking about that bullshit," she sniffed.

"What bullshit?"

"Last week's session, and I didn't come here to talk about that."

"Well, what did you come here to talk about?" he asked.

"Now, we only have fifteen minutes left, but that's not the point anyway."

"Well, what is the point, Brenda?"

"*Well*," she said, mimicking him, "we spent thirty-two minutes of *my* time talking about *you*."

"So Brenda," he said, laughing. "Let me guess. You don't want to pay for this session either?"

"Well, maybe we could prorate it."

(When Brenda brought in her payment the following week, she had an itemized account of the minutes they had spent talking about him, which she wasn't obligated to pay for.)

കൂ

Later that day, Zander strolled in twenty minutes late with something above his upper lip. Dr. Bright almost handed the boy a Kleenex because he thought it was chocolate milk. But upon closer inspection, the doctor realized it was an attempted mustache.

"So, Doc, wadja have, cancer or somethin'?" Zander asked.

"No, I had salmonella. It's like a virus in your stomach." Dr. Bright opened a bottle of water for himself and offered one to Zander, but the boy shook his head and looked at his phone.

"So, what did you do with your free afternoon last week, Zander?"

The teen looked up, "Me an' L Train got stoned in the park. Bought two hits a' acid from this dude. Tripped for three fuckin' days."

"LSD causes brain damage, you know," Dr. Bright cautioned him.

"Good," he said, looking down at his phone again.

Zander looked a little worse than the last time Dr. Bright had seen him two weeks ago. Not sick or anything, but he looked like he'd been spending more time outside. His pants were muddy, his hair was matted, and he smelled a little more like L Train.

"So, how's L Train?" Dr. Bright inquired. "Is he still kicked out of his house?"

"Nah, his mom let him come home," Zander said indifferently.

"That's good."

"Yeah, good for me. Fucker's not wearin' my clothes or stinkin' up my room anymore."

"Oh, so he was staying with you?" the doctor asked.

"Yeah, the prick. Ate us out a' house and home, too."

"Your mom doesn't mind if he stays at your place?"

Sharon's supple physique unexpectedly flooded the doctor's mind, and it took great effort to vanquish the image.

"Yeah, she minds, but she feels sorry for the fuck." Zander looked at his phone and smiled. "Speak a' the devil!" He turned the device toward Dr. Bright so that he could see L Train's name on the screen.

"Doesn't L Train know you're in a session?"

"Yeah he knows. Probably needs money or somethin'," the teen laughed.

"Do you lend him a lot of money?"

"Nah... well, we're kinda in business together." Zander's eyes rolled back, and Dr. Bright realized the boy was high.

"What kind of business are you two in together?" the doctor said, hoping to address Zander's drug use.

He coughed and laughed. "It's a private business."

It was quite obvious what his business was. However, Dr. Bright couldn't understand why Zander would talk about the drugs he did, but not about the drugs he sold.

"Selling drugs is a felony, Zander."

"Yo, man, why do you care so much?" The boy's tone darkened.

"I just don't want to see you get into any more trouble, Zander."

"How do you know my business is trouble?"

"Well, you said it was private, so..."

"So you assume it's drugs," the boy cut him off. "Yo, man, that is so fuckin' lame."

"If I'm wrong, then I'm sorry."

"Well, you are fuckin' wrong. And yo, if I wanna sit around and get accused for things, I can just hang out with my mom!"

"Does she accuse you of things, Zander?"

"What the fuck did I just say?" His eyes burned holes through the doctor. "Yo, that must feel real good being the guy askin' the questions. Shrinks, cops, parents, teachers… you guys all just sit back and ask your fuckin' questions."

"Well, do you want to ask me some questions, Zander?"

"Nah, man, I don't care about you. I just wanna live my fuckin' life. Is that so fuckin' hard to understand? And it's no fuckin' wonder I do acid. This world's so fuckin' stupid. Gotta have some escape."

"Everyone needs an escape," Dr. Bright said, suddenly feeling light-headed from his recent bout of dysentery and Zander began to laugh.

"What's so funny, Zander?"

"You are, man. You look like you need to escape more than me."

"What do you mean?" The doctor took a sip from his bottle of water.

"I dunno, Doc. You don't look so good."

"I just got over being sick and…"

"And ya gotta deal with me." The boy laughed again and then inquired nonchalantly, "Hey, Doc, what's up with that Dawn chick?"

"Dawn? Dawn who?" Chills ran down Dr. Bright's spine when Zander referred to his young client.

"That blonde with the nice tits," the boy replied.

"I don't know any…"

"Dawn Fontaine, Doc." Zander shook his head at the doctor's feeble lie.

"Oh, Dawn…"

"Yeah, the blonde with the nice tits." He repeated the lewd phrase because he saw that it made Dr. Bright uncomfortable.

"Well, Zander, I can't discuss…"

"Yeah, yeah, just thought I'd ask."

Because there were twelve million people spinning around Manhattan daily, Dr. Bright never imagined that any of his clients knew each other. When Zander mentioned Dawn, it was as if two planets had collided, and a feeling of dread began to churn in the pit of his stomach.

"Zander," the doctor asked cautiously, "how do you know Dawn?"

"Huh?" He looked up from his phone. "Oh, I seen her around the clubs."

"But you're only fifteen."

"And?"

"And clubs let you in?" the doctor asked.

"Obviously, if I go to clubs, they let me in. I mean I ain't hangin' out in the fuckin' parking lots, Doc."

"Got it. So you know her from the clubs, huh?" He continued to probe for more details about what was no doubt a toxic relationship in bloom.

"Yeah and we used a' go to the same school, but she dropped out and I got *expelled*." He stressed the last word and smiled like he was very proud of the difference.

"But, Zander, how did you know she was my client?"

"We saw each other on the street last week when you were with Sam and Ella. Don't worry, we ain't friends or nothin'."

"That would be fine with me if you were friends," Dr. Bright said, even though he didn't mean it.

"I mean, we didn't talk about you or nothin'."

"But that would be fine with me, too," he truthfully stated, since this was the least of his worries about what his two disturbed clients could spend time discussing.

"Then why'd ja lie when I asked ya about her?"

"Uh, well, I guess it just caught me off guard. I've never had a patientnquire about another patient before."

"A patient? Is that what I am? Like a psycho in a loony bin?"

"It's just a term, Zander. If it bothers you…"

He jumped out of his chair. "I'm a fuckin' mental patient!"

"Zander, if it bothers you…"

"No way, man, I like it!" Zander smiled with sickly amusement.

"Well, have a seat then."

"It's three-forty-five, man," the teen said and abruptly left.

8

It was the coldest February Manhattan had seen in eighty years with average daytime temperatures of twenty-two degrees and most nights dipping below zero. Central Park was covered in ice, subways ran on delayed schedules, buses floundered in the frozen streets, and people were advised to stay indoors. Flying home from a conference in Washington, Dr. Bright surveyed the frozen landscape from his window, and he thought that the Upper East Side with its rows of granite buildings covered in snow resembled a gigantic cemetery. Because of the slick streets, it took the cab two hours to get from JFK to his office, and as soon as he walked through the door, his phone rang.

"Doctor, where have you been?!" Louisa Fontaine screamed at him.

"I was in D.C. for a conference. Don't you remember?" Dr. Bright had made a point of telling Louisa that he'd be out of town for a week, so her amnesia surprised him.

"Didn't you get my messages, Doctor?!"

"I just walked into my office, Louisa."

"Well, it's just that Dawn has been totally out of control. Oh, Doctor Bright, I'm at my wits' end! She's been running around with this new crew, coming home at all hours of the night, doing God knows what!"

"Who's in the new crew?" the doctor inquired.

"Some troublemakers from her old school."

Zander and L Train popped into his mind.

"And on top of that, Doctor, she's dating a kid in college!"

"In college?!" Dr. Bright bellowed. "Does he know Dawn's fifteen?"

"Who knows? They just go into her room and lock the door!"

"Can't you tell her not to lock the door?" he asked.

"Oh please, Doctor. The last time I tried telling her what to do she attacked me with a knife!"

Louisa's reference to the knife incident stirred painful feelings inside Dr. Bright because he still regretted not reporting it right away.

"Can you see Dawn *today*, Doctor?" she begged.

"Our appointment is for Wednesday at four."

"Yes, but she really needs to see you today!"

"Well..." He looked for his appointment book but couldn't find it so he checked the calendar on his laptop. "No, I'm all booked, sorry."

"Couldn't you squeeze her in somewhere? What time does your last appointment end?"

"Five. Look, normally I'd..."

"This is an emergency, Doctor!" she screamed.

"I know it is, Louisa, and normally I'd have her come, but I'm booked solid the next two days. I can make our appointment earlier on Wednesday if that would help."

"Earlier? That little bitch doesn't rise till noon!"

∽

Evelyn was his first client the following day, and because he had missed their last appointment, she had a lot to tell him. First of all, there was a new man on the scene, Robert, a dentist. Dr. Bright admired the fact that all of her imaginary men were from the same economic set. There was Peter, the doctor, Martin, the lawyer, and now Robert, the dentist.

Halfway through their session, something interesting happened. Evelyn was bubbling over with all kinds of good news—Robert had cancelled a trip to Bermuda to be with her on her birthday. He had brought her chicken soup when she was sick, and had even taken her side in a dispute with his mother. Then, in the midst of all this cheer, she said, "I think I've finally found the man of my dreams." And, in an instant, her bright mood vanished. The reason for the shift was clear to Dr. Bright. She had said "man of my dreams" as a way of depicting Robert's perfection. But because all her men were from her dreams, this was a Freudian slip. A painful sliver of light had escaped from the wilderness of her delusions.

"Is everything okay, Evelyn?" Dr. Bright asked.

"I sometimes get these waves, ya know? I'll be in a perfectly good mood and then, bang."

"You'll feel sad?" the doctor inquired.

"Yeah, sad sometimes," she replied.

"What else?" he asked.

"Angry sometimes… anxious. Sometimes all three at the same time."

"What are you feeling right now, Evelyn?"

"What am I feeling right now?" She looked down into her purse, "I guess I'm feeling angry, Doctor."

"Do you know what you're angry about?"

"No. That's why I call them waves. They're sudden and strong and they come out of nowhere."

Dr. Bright was positive that Evelyn was angry at him for evoking the painful, yet still-not-accepted-truth about Robert. This made him reflect on one of the tenets of counseling—because pain is an integral part of the healing process, clients naturally associate therapy with suffering. Some even see their therapist as the source of the pain, despite the fact that their wounds were carved long ago.

"Evelyn, I'm sure it feels like they come out of nowhere, but I bet something triggers them."

"I disagree, Doctor, because they happen at all different times of the day," she said, closing her purse. "And they happen all over the place. In the car, in the shower, in the park, everywhere, and the season doesn't matter, either. Spring, summer, winter, fall… cloudy, rainy, sunny. That's why I call them waves, Doctor, because…"

"Okay, Evelyn," he said, cutting her off. "Let's talk about this last wave."

"Fine," she said defensively.

"Now, we were talking about Robert…"

"Oh, it has nothing to do with him."

"I'm not saying it does," he continued. "I'm just trying to figure out what triggered the anger."

"Does something have to trigger it? Maybe it's just a part of me. Like when you suddenly realize you're tired. Nothing triggers it, you're just tired."

"Evelyn, why are you so resistant to…"

"Because you're trying to blame it on Robert!" She burst into tears.

"Evelyn," he said, making his voice soft. "I'm not saying it has anything to do with Robert…"

"Yes, you are!" Mascara drained down her cheeks.

"I'm just trying to figure out…"

"Bullshit!" She tore a tissue from the box of Kleenex on his desk. "Ya know," she said, wiping her eyes, "I think I might have to get a new therapist. Because, I mean, isn't the point of therapy to make you feel better?"

"Well… Evelyn… eventually, yes."

"But I always leave here feeling worse. Is that normal, Doctor?"

"No, that's no good. Maybe we should talk about it."

"I thought we were talking about it," she quipped.

"Yes… good point… I meant maybe we should talk about it in more detail. What do you want out of therapy, Evelyn?"

"*What do I want out of therapy?*" she said with crimson indignation. "I've been your client for two whole years and now you're asking me this?"

"No, actually, I asked you when you first started."

"So why ask me again?"

"Because I want to see if your goals are still the same," he rejoined.

"Oh, like you remember them, Doctor," she said incredulously.

He spun around, opened his cabinet, and pulled out Evelyn's file.

"You keep that stuff on file?" she asked.

"Of course." He looked down at his notes. "Now, do you remember what your goals were?"

"No." She adjusted her bra. "Can you give me a hint?"

"Well, you had just left Sheering and Gleason…"

"Left? You mean I was fired," she said, laughing a little.

"Do you remember why you were fired?"

"Remember?! That's when I couldn't leave my house! I missed thirty-three days of work, and when I didn't show up for that important hearing, they fired me."

"And do you remember what your goals were then?"

"Well, one of them must've been getting a job." She laughed. "I mean you're not gonna last long in Manhattan without a job."

"Anything else?" Dr. Bright asked.

"Well…" Her smile faded. "Getting rid of that crippling anxiety."

"That's right. We started with phone sessions, remember?"

"Yes," she said, looking out the window.

"And your first goal was to get here once a week."

"I forgot about that." She pulled her tissue apart. "I suppose I ought to thank you."

"Thank me? Thank yourself. You've done all the work."

"Yes, but I couldn't have done it without you, Doctor."

"No. That's not true. Therapy is all about a person's willingness to change."

Evelyn looked down at the torn tissue in her hand as Dr. Bright continued.

"And I don't care if the therapist is Sigmund Freud. If the client doesn't have the motivation and courage to change, then nothing's going to change."

9

Winter disappeared overnight, and the next day was spring. Temperatures soared into the seventies. Birds filled the turquoise sky. Dr. Bright went out on his balcony to admire the sudden beauty. Then, he went inside and turned on the TV for a weather report to make sure it was real. But all they kept showing were aerial views of Central Park Lake, and when the images shifted to police divers, body bags, and barking dogs, he turned it off. He didn't want to stain the lovely Monday morning with an all-too-gruesome, all-too-common New York story.

Alex, a new client, was thirty-five years old, portly and single. He always wore exercise clothes and talked about losing weight, but he also carried a surfeit of candy in his pocket which he ate throughout his sessions. Despite his ambivalence in some matters, he had one goal that was crystal clear—he wanted to find a girlfriend. However, on this particular morning, he was preoccupied with other matters.

"Isn't it just terrible, Doctor?"

"Isn't what terrible, Alex?"

"What happened last night to that man in Central Park."

Dr. Bright recalled the aerial views of the Lake. "Oh, I didn't really catch it."

"Don't you read the papers? It's been in all the papers," Alex said with an admonishing tone.

"I usually do, but today I didn't," the doctor replied.

"Well, you're lucky, Doctor. It was awful." Alex took a Tootsie Roll out of his pocket and began unwrapping it. "I always eat when I'm upset."

"Well, let's talk about why you're upset."

He put the Tootsie Roll in his mouth and said with palpable irritation, "Didn't I just tell you?"

"No… you mean that thing in Central Park?" Dr. Bright asked.

"Yes!"

"Well, you started to, but…"

"A man was stabbed to death and thrown into the Lake by West Seventy-second Street," Alex said, swallowing. "And I go there all the time with my dogs!"

"That's terrible," the doctor rejoined.

His client continued. "They said he was stabbed fifty times and that one of his hands was missing."

"Jesus," Dr. Bright said. "Probably some gang thing."

"Yes! The Latin Kings! And I go there all the time with my dogs!"

After his appointment with Alex, Dr. Bright bought a newspaper and the images of Central Park Lake he'd seen on television earlier that day dominated the front page—"Slash Frenzy" relayed the grisly murder of Michael Miller, also known as "Mickey," a forty-year-old resident of Manhattan's Upper West Side. According to reports, there had been repeated stab wounds, intestines falling from a slashed abdomen, and a severed hand. To most New Yorkers, *where* it had happened was more terrifying than *what* had happened—gruesome murders were commonplace in the "outer boroughs," but the fact that this happened in Central Park, the crowning jewel of Manhattan, sent a shudder of fear through the city. The writer concluded by saying that the killing "appeared to be gang-related," but authorities were still gathering evidence.

On page three, a picture of the yellow king Dr. Bright had seen in the subway several months ago captured his attention. According to the article, gangs had accounted for forty percent of New York's homicides last year, and while Miller's slaying was horrendous, it was part of an upward trend of gang violence in the city. Beneath the article, there was a map showing the city's myriad "turf boundaries," and Dr. Bright realized that Manhattan was infested by Bloods, Brims, Crips, MS-13 members, and Latin Kings. There was also a web address to an online interactive "gang map," but Dr. Bright had seen enough crime for one day.

ↇ

Dawn walked in twenty-minutes late with music blasting out of her earbuds. When Dr. Bright asked her to turn it down she reluctantly acquiesced, but he could still hear the muffled concert, so he asked her to put her phone away. With her eyes glued to his, she pressed the power button, plucked the buds out of her ears and placed the cord around her neck.

"So, what has Fatso been saying about me?" Dawn asked.

"Are you referring to your mother?"

"Don't give me that crap, Doctor. I can always tell when you two have been talking shit about me."

"How can you tell?" The doctor inquired.

"Because you're like, *Dawn, turn your phone off,*" she mimicked him.

"Is it really that important for you to have it on?" he asked.

"Yeah it fucking is!" she said, suddenly furious, shaking the dead phone at him. "How'd you feel if I fucking turned you off?!"

"Well, I don't know. I'd be turned off," Dr. Bright said, making light of her threat. "But, go ahead and turn it back on if you really want to."

Dawn restored power, and as soon as the apple icon illuminated, her anger vanished. She studied the doctor with a curious smile on her face. "So that's it?" she asked, as if some deep mystery had just been solved.

"What is it, Dawn?"

"You think you can turn me on and off."

"What do you mean?" Dr. Bright inquired.

"You know, like Simon Says."

"Simon Says?" he asked.

"Watch." She sat up straight. "Simon Says turn off." She closed her eyes and let her arms fall to her sides. "Simon Says turn on." She opened her eyes and waved her arms in the air.

Dr. Bright was about to address her analogy when her phone chimed. "Oh, my God!" She laughed. "That is *too* funny!"

"What is it, Dawn?"

She ignored the doctor's query and began typing a reply. She sat back in her chair and continued typing. "That is too fucking funny."

"What's funny, Dawn?"

"Do you *really* want to know?" she asked whimsically.

"Sure." He played along.

"Okay, I'll give you a hint. I just got a text from someone we both know."

He considered playing dumb about their mutual acquaintance but decided against it. "Is it Zander?"

"Zander?!" she exclaimed incredulously. "Nope, not Zander. Guess again."

"Not Zander?" he asked. "Was it your mother?"

"Nope, it wasn't Fatso. Guess again."

"Your father?"

"Nope!"

"Well, Dawn, I'm pretty sure I've accounted for…" Dr. Bright began.

"You're not trying hard enough," she urged him. "Close your eyes and don't open them till I say so. Okay?"

"Okay," he acquiesced.

"Now," she said in a silken voice, "think of all the people we could possibly know."

He watched Zander, Louisa, and Howard tumble around in his mind like laundry.

"Okay," Dawn said after a minute. "Simon Says open your eyes."

He looked at her. "Sorry, Dawn. I still have the same possibilities."

"Oh, Doctor," the girl said mournfully while gathering her belongings. "I don't think I want to play with you anymore." She put in her earbuds and texted for the remainder of their session.

The phone rang right after Dawn left, and Dr. Bright assumed it was Louisa calling to check in. However, he was happily surprised to hear Sharon's voice on the other end of the line. She was calling to cancel Zander's appointment because he was sick. Then, she asked the doctor if he was willing to make a house-call because, apparently, Zander really wanted to see him. As he was attempting to digest her request, Sharon started laughing.

"I know, I know," she said ironically. "The boy who has to be dragged to your office wants to see you."

Dr. Bright laughed as well and then he noticed that the appointment book he'd lost several weeks ago was right there on his desk.

"How does tomorrow at three-thirty work for you?" he asked while thumbing through the pages of the recovered register.

Here, Sharon described Zander's "mono-like" symptoms, and she explained that they were going to the doctor in the morning to have him tested. She cautioned the doctor about the possible threat of contagion.

"I think it will be fine as long as we don't kiss," he said in gest. But, when he didn't hear the laugh, he had expected he thought she'd misconstrued his meaning and he tried to fix his failed joke. "I meant as long as Zander and I didn't kiss… I didn't mean you and me…"

"I know what you meant, silly," she said in a comforting voice. "I was just checking my calendar to see if tomorrow works and it does. See you soon!"

After they hung up, Dr. Bright realized he was blushing.

∾

Dr. Bright bought a newspaper the next day and the headline "Central Park Slaying Suspect Questioned by Police" caught his attention. Allegedly, Angel Valdez, a high-ranking member of the Latin Kings had been seen by several witnesses having a "heated discussion" with Mickey Miller a few weeks before his brutal murder.

Their dispute, according to reports, had been over drugs. The article went on to say that Valdez was also being questioned about Tiny Lopez, a drug dealer, who police had found in a dumpster last December with a bullet in his head. Apparently, Lopez and Miller had been selling marijuana and cocaine in Latin Kings' territory and this, it seemed, had led to their demise. Curiously, however, the article concluded by saying that authorities weren't convinced that Miller's murder was gang-related.

After reading the paper, Dr. Bright felt an odd mixture of solace and terror—knowing authorities were close to cracking the case brought relief but seeing Manhattan's dark underbelly exposed like this was unsettling, for he realized how thin the veil was that separated the city's sparkling façade from its gory entrails—seconds away from the bright lights of Broadway, dead men in dumpsters stared up at the stars.

At three o'clock, Dr. Bright hailed a cab and headed to Zander's apartment in the East Sixties. It was a pale brownstone with wisteria climbing the walls. Sharon was waiting in the hallway when the doctor reached the third floor. Wearing black leggings and a lilac hoodie, she looked like she had just come back from the gym.

"How is Zander?" Dr. Bright asked.

"Not good," she whispered. "The mono tests came back negative."

"Well, that's good, right?" he inquired.

"Yes, but something's wrong with him."

"There's a flu going around," the doctor offered.

"No, it's not that. It's something else." She checked the empty stairwell. "Last night I heard him crying and when I checked on him he was asleep."

"Well, sometimes with a fever…"

"No, no," she cut him off. "I've nursed him through a thousand fevers, and this is different."

The doctor probed, "How long has he been like this?"

"A few days. He spent the night at a friend's house last weekend and when he came home he looked like crap. Anyway," she said, opening the door, "come on in. He's waiting for you."

They entered the apartment, a cozy two-bedroom with bay windows, high ceilings and hardwood floors. Sharon led Dr. Bright down a hallway until they reached a closed door.

"Zander?" She knocked. "Dr. Bright's here."

"Okay," a feint voice replied from within.

She looked at Dr. Bright with moist eyes then opened the door. Zander was playing a game on his phone when they entered. In his New York Yankees pajamas, he looked twelve-years old, and he didn't look sick. In fact, he had never looked healthier.

"Can I get you two anything?" Sharon asked.

"No mom. We're good," her son replied.

"Okay." She glanced once more at the doctor before walking out and closing the door.

"How's it going, Zander?" Dr. Bright asked.

"You can sit over there if you want, Doc." Zander pointed to a chair piled high with folded laundry. "Just throw that crap on the floor."

Dr. Bright walked over, carefully placed the clothes on a desk by the window, and sat down. "How are you feeling, Zander?" His query was followed by a silence so complete that not even the hum of traffic, indigenous to Manhattan, could be heard. "It's nice and quiet here," the doctor commented.

"Yeah, man. Too fucking quiet," Zander said, putting his phone away. "It's like a fucking tomb."

"Well," said Dr. Bright, thinking of the fire engines that raced up and down his street all night, "I like it."

"That's cuz you ain't got a lotta shit on your mind," the boy said.

"Well, that's true," the doctor replied thoughtfully. "So, what's on your mind, Zander?"

"Aw man," the teen responded in a vapid voice. "I don't know where to begin."

Dr. Bright let the silence work its magic for a moment before saying, "Pick one thing that's bothering you and tell me about it."

"One thing?" Zander sat up and looked around the room. "Okay I got one. So, is the stuff I tell you just between us? You know? Like confident, or whatever the fuck that word is?"

"Yes, Zander. Everything you tell me is confidential."

"No matter what?" Zander asked with marked concern.

"Yes. Everything you tell me is private. There are only a few exceptions."

The boy sat up. "Like what?"

"I'm required by law to report domestic abuse or neglect."

"So, like if some dad is beating the crap out of his kid or some shit like that?" Zander asked.

"Yes, I'd have to report that."

"Anything else, Doc?"

"Well," the doctor continued, "I'd report information to protect the public from serious harm."

"You mean like if some dude talked about killing people or blowing up a building?" the teen inquired.

"Yes, I'd want to report that."

"Well," Zander's voice trembled a bit, "what if someone already did something bad and it was like over?"

"I'm not required to report things that happened in the past, unless they're part of an ongoing pattern," Dr. Bright explained.

"So," the boy continued, "if a dude told you he blew up a building and he was gonna blow up another you'd snitch on him?"

"Yes," Dr. Bright replied. "I'd release the information to protect the public from harm."

"Okay, okay," Zander said with mounting eagerness. "But what if the dude felt really bad about the building and he didn't want to blow up another? Would you still have to rat him out?"

"No, Zander. I wouldn't rat him out."

Zander took a swig off the Gatorade on his nightstand and said, "Hey, Doc, can ya do me a favor?"

"Of course."

"Can ya open up those for me?" the boy said, referring to the closed window blinds.

"Certainly." The doctor twisted the wooden wand and the room filled with light.

"Can ya crack the window too, Doc?"

"Sure." Dr. Bright opened it and a soft breeze slipped in.

"Fuckin nice outside, huh?" Zander asked.

"Yes, it's beautiful," the doctor responded.

"I ain't been outside since Sunday," the teen said in a grave voice. "Today's Thursday, right, Doc?"

"Yes, Zander. Today is Thursday."

"Four fuckin days," Zander said while rubbing his eyes.

"So, Zander," Dr. Bright began after a moment, "what happened last Sunday?"

"Last Sunday?" the teen inquired. "Nothing. Why?"

"Well, it's obvious that something occurred," Dr. Bright pushed.

"Nothing fuckin happened last Sunday," Zander whispered loudly. "What the fuck are you talking about?"

"Something scared you last Sunday, Zander."

"Nothing fuckin scared me!"

"Really?" Dr. Bright challenged. "Then why have you been hiding in your room since then?"

Zander gripped the Gatorade bottle with both hands and glared at the doctor with pitch black eyes; he seemed on the verge of violence. His anger dissipated and he fell back onto his pillows. "It wasn't Sunday," he said in a thin voice. "It was Saturday."

"All right," Dr. Bright said softly, "so what happened?"

"I can't tell you, Doc."

"Why   not?" Stillness strangled the room until Zander said, "Cuz it's too fuckin' awful."

"Nothing is too awful to talk about, Zander. Every problem can be solved."

"Not this one, Doc." The teen stared at the ceiling with terror in his eyes as if a legion of demons with pitchforks were up there waiting to pounce on him.

"Listen, Zander. When we bury our problems, they gather strength. When we talk about them, they fade and become manageable. You can tell me anything."

Zander looked around as if he was searching for the right words to begin his disclosure until a deafening siren from a passing police car tore the room in half. When the sound finally faded, the boy sat up with a cynical smile and said, "Time to wrap it up, right, Doc?"

"No, we've got a few more minutes," Dr. Bright said while glancing at his watch.

"Nah, that's okay," the boy replied. "Plus, I ain't ready to talk about this shit anyway."

"All right, Zander." The doctor rose from his chair. "Maybe you'll tell me about it next week."

"Something tells me you're already gonna know about it by then, Doc," Zander said ominously as he picked up his phone and resumed his game.

Dr. Bright walked over and opened the door. "See you soon, Zander."

"Bye, Doc."

Sharon was in the kitchen taking a tray of cookies out of the oven when Dr. Bright emerged. She had showered, and in her t-shirt and faded jeans she looked sexy. "Oh, Doctor!" she exclaimed. "I didn't see you there."

"We just finished," he replied nervously.

"Can you sit for a minute?"

"Yes, I have a little time," he said, even though Zander was his last client of the day and he had plenty of time.

"These need to cool off." Sharon pointed to the cookies. "But I just made a fresh pot of coffee. Would you like some?"

"Sure," Dr. Bright replied.

"Well, come here then." She invited him into the snug kitchen and pointed to the accessories on the counter. "Cups, creamer, sugar, spoons. Help yourself."

The flowery smell of her freshly-washed hair flustered Dr. Bright and he dropped his spoon.

"Here, let me help you with that." Sharon picked up the fallen utensil and moved close to him. "Cream and sugar?" she asked.

"Yes please."

Her arm brushed his hand while she was stirring his coffee. He was deeply aroused by the touch of her skin, and he immediately felt guilty because this was the mother of a client who just happened to be going through an emotional crisis down the hall. Fortunately, she carried his cup to the table or he probably would've dropped that too.

"So, how is he?" Sharon inquired when they were seated.

"He's working through something," the doctor replied and sipped his coffee.

"Working through something?" she asked skeptically.

"Yes, I think so, but the good news is he's not sick."

"Well, I knew *that*," she said, slightly annoyed. "So, what is it?"

"I'm not sure."

"Do you think he's in trouble, Doctor?"

"Well," he sipped his coffee again, "I don't know if he's in trouble, but he's extremely worried about something."

"But you don't know what it is?"

"No, Sharon, I honestly don't."

She looked around the room with a storm in her eyes. "Ever since he came home last Sunday, he's been a different kid. He won't eat, he won't talk, he won't leave the house." Two tears slipped down her cheeks. "And I don't know what to do."

"Well," Dr. Bright began softly, "he's getting ready to talk about it, which is a good sign."

"How do you know?" Sharon whispered.

"Because, whatever it is, I don't think he can hold it in much longer."

She wiped her tears away and said in a measured voice, "He's done something horrible, hasn't he?"

After a moment the doctor replied, "He's done something he shouldn't have done."

Sharon stood up and walked into the kitchen. Then she began transferring the cookies into a Tupperware container. "These are for you," she said gently.

The doctor followed her. "That was nice of you."

She took a step toward him and looked deeply into his eyes. "It's you who's nice."

Then, as if they'd been intimate for years, they fell into each other's arms and shared a passionate embrace. Dr.

Bright was aware of the fact that their hug breached every ethical boundary in the book, but with her warm body against his and redolent scent of her hair in his nostrils, he didn't care—he just wanted to hold her forever. And walking down Sixty-second Street later with a container of cookies in his hands, he knew he was falling in love.

❧

Dr. Bright couldn't remember his dreams when he woke but they must have been about Sharon because he found himself immersed in that state of pure joy only new love can bring—his coffee tasted perfect, his clothes felt brand new, and the din of traffic below sounded like a symphony. At one point, he began to call her. But, before he finished dialing, the impossibility of the situation occurred to him and he hung up—dating his client's mother clearly violated the code of conduct; even their embrace last night had been an ethical transgression. He tried to put it behind him.

While getting dressed for the day, Dr. Bright examined his dilemma, and after a few mental maneuvers, he started to feel better—their embrace had been platonic, he told himself. It had been intimate and affectionate, but not romantic, and even though his emotions protested, he beat them down with rationalizations until he felt convinced. However, as he was leaving his apartment, he saw Sharon's cookies on the counter, his amorous feelings for her returned, and the inner conflict started all over again. Fortunately, Dr. Bright could count on a busy day to distract him from his troubles.

Alex, his first client of the day, was waiting for him on the stoop, and, as usual, he talked a mile a minute as the doctor picked up his mail and opened the door. Today, his client's discourse focused on the developments in the Central Park murder case.

"Anyway," Alex said after taking a sip off the Hydro-Flask he always carried with him, "it was all about drugs."

"Yes," Dr. Bright replied, "I read about that yesterday."

"And they said Miller lived on the Upper West Side, but they didn't say where."

"Well," the doctor began, "his address is private information."

"But that's where I live!" his client protested.

Alex measured all things in terms of their relationship to him—the slaying in Strawberry Fields was significant because he walked his dogs there; Mickey Miller's address mattered because they might have shared a zip code. Dr. Bright also noticed that Alex tended to focus on peripheral events to avoid the holes in his life, particularly the abject loneliness that had driven him to therapy.

"And, Doctor, did you read about that man they found in the dumpster?"

"Yes, I did," the doctor rejoined, "but I really wanted to hear how your date went last weekend."

Alex looked down and began playing with the zipper on his jacket. "Not very well," he said after a moment. "Turns out she wasn't Jewish."

Alex had been using *JDate*, an online dating service for Jewish singles; apparently, however, non-Jews used it as well.

"I mean, did she have to wait till the crème brulee arrived to tell me she was a gentile?" He took a Tootsie Roll out of his pocket, unwrapped it, and ate it in one bite.

Dr. Bright had cautioned Alex about the dangers of dinner as a first date. The time commitment created unnecessary pressures, and he had suggested meeting for coffee, but Alex had disregarded his advice and made reservations at The Boathouse, a trendy restaurant in Central Park.

"Well, was she nice at least?" Dr. Bright asked.

"Megan? Oh, she was great." Alex brightened. "She's cute, funny, kind, and she likes everything I like—gardening, cooking, and board games, and she even has three Shih Tzus—Penelope, Sage, and Max," he smiled at their names.

"So, are you going to call her?" the doctor inquired.

"No, I'm not going to call her," he snapped.

"Why not?"

"Because she's not Jewish!" He took out another Tootsie Roll and ate it.

Alex was adamant about finding a Jewish girlfriend, even though he hardly ever attended temple and had long since abandoned most of the traditions.

"Why is her religion so important to you, Alex?" Dr. Bright asked.

"Because I'm Jewish, and I want a Jewish girlfriend!" he exclaimed with scarlet anger.

"Right. I got that," the doctor said dispassionately, "but you told me you didn't believe in God."

"SHHHHH!" Alex crouched and looked nervously around the room because the God he didn't believe in might be listening. "Don't say it like that," he whispered.

"Why not?" Dr. Bright probed.

Alex straightened up. "Anyway, it's not about the God stuff, it's about the traditions."

"Like what?"

"There's shabbat, tefillin, mezuzah, brachot…" He scanned his mind for more. "And anyway," he said after a few moments, "those are important."

"Yes, I'm sure they are," the doctor affirmed, "and you could teach her about all of them."

"Well, I suppose I could." Alex considered the idea for a moment, and then said, "But she's a liar."

"A liar?" Dr. Bright said incredulously. "What did she lie about?"

"About being Jewish!" his client bawled.

"Alex, did she ever say she was Jewish?"

"No, but she's using *JDate*, and that website is for Jews," he said with conviction.

"Maybe she registered as a non-Jew. People do that, don't they?"

"Yes, they do, but she didn't," Alex replied and then added proudly, "I'm very meticulous, Doctor. I scrutinize the profiles of potential suitors."

"Yes, I'm sure you do, Alex. But isn't it possible that you overlooked it?"

"Fine." He pulled out his phone. "I'll prove it to you." He tapped the screen a few times, and then his face turned to stone. "Shit."

"What's the matter, Alex?"

"You're right." He turned his phone toward the doctor. "She registered as a non-Jew."

"Well, that's good," Dr. Bright said blithely. "Cute, kind, funny, and *honest*," he emphasized the last word. "Sounds like a keeper to me."

Alex looked out the window, and his face became a painting of sorrow. "Doctor," he said after a moment, "did you ever want someone badly, but know it was wrong?"

The question pierced the wall that kept Dr. Bright's personal thoughts at bay, and Sharon flooded his being— he smelled her freshly-washed hair, felt the supple contours of her body, and his mood darkened with the realization that last night's embrace would be the pinnacle of their impossible relationship.

"Yes, Alex," he replied with a heavy heart. "I have."

"What did you do about it?!" Alex asked with urgency.

"Well…" Dr. Bright used all of skills to vanquish the specter of Sharon. "I weighed the pros and cons of the situation. Here." He took a legal pad and pen out of his drawer and handed them to Alex. "Make a list." He instructed his client to write the advantages of pursuing a relationship with Megan on one side of the page and the disadvantages on the other side. And while Alex itemized, Dr. Bright briefly considered his situation with Sharon again and a grim feeling of closure gripped his heart when he realized that the disadvantages—jeopardizing his career and his professional relationship with Zander—clearly trumped the advantages of being with Sharon.

"Okay, here." Alex handed him the legal pad covered in chaotic script. "It didn't help."

"Why not?" the doctor asked.

"Look!" he cried and handed the legal pad to his therapist who examined the document. The left side of the page marked "cons" contained a few items about Judaism while the right side of the page marked "pros" was packed with bright adjectives and cheerful phrases pertaining to Megan that spilled over into the margins.

"But, Alex," Dr. Bright remarked, "this is wonderful."

"Wonderful?" his client parried. "It's awful."

"Why is it awful?"

"Because I promised my mother I'd marry a Jewish girl."

His mother now lived in Palm Springs with her third husband, and Alex had described her as a self-centered diva who cared about two things—herself and herself. In fact, they rarely spoke, so Dr. Bright was skeptical about his client's desires to please her. Furthermore, he knew that Alex's criteria for a potential suitor had nothing to do with his mother at all. Rather, it was a manifestation of the contract with loneliness he had signed with himself—deep down, Alex didn't like Alex, so depriving himself of love was an act of revenge, and Dr. Bright had to help this man resurrect his buried self-esteem.

✃

A golden glow had settled on the Upper East Side as Dr. Bright walked home that evening. As he passed the sidewalk cafes teeming with smiling couples, a spear of sadness went through him because the weekend had come—during the week he could count on work to distract him from his isolation, but Friday evening marked the beginning of a solitary journey into the recesses of himself. He would, of course, conjure events to keep his loneliness at bay—he'd have his morning coffee surrounded by cordial strangers at Starbucks, he'd go to a museum in the afternoon and attend a performance at the Lincoln Center at night, but all of this required energy, and if he paused or took a breath, his solitude wrapped around him like a moth-eaten shawl.

As he waited for the light to change at Eighty-fourth Street, he thought of all the advice he'd given over the years to clients struggling with the aftershocks of divorce—let yourself mourn, avoid alcohol, wait a year before dating again. Well, he had grieved, he didn't drink, the year had passed, and his only romance had been a furtive embrace with his client's mother, a dalliance which had been destined to fail. Then, he recalled a conversation he'd had with Alex at the close of today's session and the embers of enlightenment began to glow inside of him.

"Doctor, why am I so unhappy?" Alex asked.

"Because you're punishing yourself," Dr. Bright replied.

"Punishing myself?!" his client cried incredulously. *"But I'm being nice to myself."*

"How?" the doctor probed. "Tell me about it."

"I'm exercising and dating online. I'm really putting myself out there."

"Okay." Dr. Bright glanced at the notebook that lay open on his lap. "Let's consider your dates so far." He turned a few pages. "Ah, yes. There was Liz, the lady from Wisconsin."

"What's wrong with that?" Alex asked defensively. "We shared the same interests."

"Wisconsin is nine hundred miles away," Dr. Bright shot back." That's what's wrong with it."

"Uh, in case you hadn't realized it before, Doctor," his client said bitterly. "There are these little things called airplanes."

"Ah, yes," Dr. Bright parried, "so you're going to take a three-hour flight every time you want to see her?"

"Well, she could fly here too," Alex's tone softened as his stance began to crumble.

"Alex, come on," the doctor rebuked him.

"Okay, okay, you're right. But what about Nancy? She was nice."

"Nancy?!" Dr. Bright exclaimed. "The sanitation worker from Queens?"

"What's wrong with sanitation workers? They keep the city clean."

"Alex, there's nothing wrong with sanitation workers," the doctor replied. "But you're an interior decorator. What the heck would you two talk about?"

"We could talk about Queens," Alex offered. "It's not just a bedroom community anymore."

"Have you ever been there?" Dr. Bright asked.

"I went to a Mets game when I was a kid."

"Great," the doctor replied dispassionately. "And after you discussed Shea Stadium, what would you talk about?"

"Oh, I don't know," his client's voice had become misty and distant. "I believe in recycling. It's good for the planet."

Dr. Bright paused to let the silence form a gentle transition, and then said, "Alex, do you see what I mean? With Liz there was distance, with Nancy there was vocation, and with Megan there's religion. Each girl was carefully picked for her incompatibilities."

"Yes, doctor," his client sadly replied. "I see what you mean. I'm picking them because I know they won't work. But why am I doing that?"

"Because you don't believe you deserve love in your life."

A flourish of car horns awoke Dr. Bright from his reflections, and he found himself standing in front of his apartment building. And, gazing up at the forty-story tower, he wondered if he hadn't been following his client's pattern of punishment—he, too, was terribly lonely, and like Alex he had chosen a deliberately unattainable companion to fall for. As the doctor arrived at this conclusion, he reached into his pocket and realized he'd left his keys in his office, so he turned around and walked back. Luckily, Antonio, the building's super, was there to let him in.

As Dr. Bright grabbed the golden pile of keys on his desk and turned to leave, the phone rang. Figuring it might be Louisa calling to complain or Brenda with a bill clenched in her fist, he started towards the door, but his conscience got the better of him and he picked up the receiver.

"Doctor, it's Sharon. I'm so glad I caught you!" Her lovely voice instantly filled the depths of his heart with light.

"Hello Sharon." He tried to mask his joy. "Is everything okay? How's Zander?"

"Oh, he's fine," she replied. "Turns out his little sickness was all about a girl."

Dr. Bright had a sinking feeling that the girl she was referring to was Dawn, but because ethics prevented him from sharing anything, he offered a bland reply. "Well, that's good to hear."

"Yeah, they broke up and he was pretty upset but you know how teenagers are."

"Oh, yes," returned Dr. Bright. "I do."

Sharon said, "Turns out he was with her last weekend, and then they had some kind of argument, but now it's over."

Dr. Bright didn't believe that a spat had been the sole cause of Zander's recent bout of depression, but he refrained from further inquiry.

"Anyway," she took a breath and continued, "my yoga studio has a booth at the Lexington Street Fair tomorrow and we're giving away free passes and Jamba Juice coupons and I was wondering if you wanted to stop by."

Her invitation caught him off guard and he fumbled with a series of beginnings, "Um... I... well..."

"Hey!" Sharon cut him off. "You said you wanted to try yoga, right? Well, here's your chance."

Dr. Bright recalled his casual reference to yoga, and he felt compelled to accept her invitation. "Um... okay... what time?" "Well," she replied, "the street fair goes from eleven to four, so stop by anytime."

"Okay," he responded.

"We can grab a Jamba Juice afterwards, if you want to," she added hopefully.

"That sounds great, Sharon."

"Cool," she said. "See you tomorrow."

"See you tomorrow," Dr. Bright rejoined, and as he slowly hung up, it occurred to him that he'd just been asked out on a date. Suddenly, the grim musings about doomed romances that had tumbled around in his mind all day vanished because of one irrefutable fact—*she* had asked him out, which meant that the attraction was mutual and not a phantom feeling conjured by his mind. However, running parallel to his joy was the troubling realization that he'd just agreed to have a date with Zander's mother. He actually picked up the phone to cancel, but another thought occurred to him, and he put the receiver down—he could clean up the whole mess by visiting her tent tomorrow, engaging in platonic platitudes, and leaving. This would be an appropriate course of action that distanced him from last night's transgression, and it would also give him something to do.

10

Dr. Bright awoke to a lovely spring morning—the sun wandered in and out of creamy clouds, and from his terrace he could see a ring of pink cherry blossoms at the entrance of Central Park. He normally bought a newspaper and went to Starbucks on Saturday mornings, but today, he was content to have his coffee at home.

Saturday mornings was also the time he devoted to reviewing the notes taken in therapy sessions during the past week. They provided insight on patients' progress and often shaped the direction of future sessions. Looking back, he could see that last week had been eventful, but this was often the case when the weather changed, especially when spring showed up after a long, cold winter—it was as if his clients' problems mirrored the roots and vines that lay dormant beneath the frozen soil because when spring arrived they blossomed with a yearning to be recognized.

While perusing his notes he remembered the Central Park slaying that had stunned the city, and how it had affected Alex who lived only blocks from the scene of the crime. Then, he recalled their conversation about incompatible partners and self-inflicted loneliness, and he began constructing a course of action to help Alex like Alex that included prioritizing himself and plenty of self-praise.

Next, he reviewed his notes on Dawn, and he reflected on the ferocious fit she'd thrown after being asked to turn off her phone. He had seen her angry before, but in the past her ire had been contained; whereas this time her fury had been naked and menacing, and although her threat to "turn him off" had been indirect, it was bordering on reportable. After that, he reflected on his trip to Zander's apartment—his young client hiding out in his room was a spectacle of paranoia, and although Sharon had said that a rift had been the cause of it, Dr. Bright wasn't satisfied because he had counseled hundreds of clients going through breakups. Zander's demeanor didn't denote heartbreak; rather, it resembled the ravaging effects of guilt, and Dr. Bright was convinced that his young client had done something illegal. While he tried to avoid speculation, he was fairly certain that Zander's misconduct had something to do with drugs—in the past month the boy's disposition had darkened and he'd made several references to narcotics including a fledgling "business" with L Train that could only mean trouble.

When Dr. Bright finished reviewing his notes, it was two o'clock, so he began preparing to go to the street fair. After rejecting several outfits, it occurred to him that he was nervous—for, even though his mind was planning on a brief, friendly visit, void of romantic intentions, in his heart it felt like a date. Adding to his discomfort, one of the discarded shirts on the bed was a present from his daughter and a wave of guilt washed over him. He and Zoe always had a special relationship—their bond was more akin to best friends than father-daughter. They shared the same sense of humor, the same temperament, and they were close confidants. Margot had been a loving mother and a loyal wife, but she was prone to bouts of anxiety and preserving her peace of mind had become a top priority for Dr. Bright and Zoe, even if it meant keeping secrets from her. For example, when the vengeful headmaster of Trinity Prep had threatened to suspend the precocious teen because she had ditched school to attend the Yankees World Series Parade, Dr. Bright fabricated a tale about giving her permission to go, and the whole thing faded before it reached Margot's ears. Besides, he had raised Zoe to be a Yankees' fan—they had gone to dozens of games together, including game six of the fall classic where Hideki Matsui's six RBIs slammed the door on the Phillies, so in his mind attending the parade had been Zoe's birthright. As he was reflecting on more of his daughter's innocuous infractions and their comical coverups, the phone rang, and hoping it was her, he answered with a delighted heart, but the telemarketer's mechanical voice dampened his hopes. After getting rid of the solicitor, he called Zoe, but it went straight to voicemail, so he left her a message.

Lexington Avenue was usually a sea of strangled traffic accompanied by blaring horns and shouted curses that drifted through the dirty air. However, between Seventy-second and Eighty-sixth Streets, the old thoroughfare was packed with colorful tents, prismatic streamers, and pedestrians. Dr. Bright hadn't been to a street fair in many years, and it occurred to him that finding Sharon might be difficult because there were hundreds of vendors, and he didn't even know the name of her yoga studio. Furthermore, it was three-thirty, so he only had half an hour to find her.

He walked toward Seventy-second Street through the crowd of sun-dazed spectators hoping to catch a glimpse of her, but by the time he reached the end of the venue where traffic flowed freely, it was almost four o'clock. Turning around and looking back with a pocketful of dwindling hopes, he realized how much he'd been counting on seeing her because the thought of not seeing her made him mildly nauseous.

Many of the merchants were beginning to pack up their wares as he walked north through the thinning crowd, and just when his disappointment had begun to congeal, he spied a small turquoise tent with a banner that read BREATHE wrapped around it. He realized that he hadn't seen it before because it had been squashed between two gigantic pizza pavilions that were now being dismantled. As he approached, he saw Sharon gathering brochures and putting them in a box. She was wearing faded jeans with aqua tank top with a golden wave of hair swept to one side. It occurred to him that the picture of her he'd been carrying in his mind couldn't compare with the reality of her beauty. And just as he was admiring her lovely face and the curves of her toned body, Sharon looked up at him with a coy smile.

"Bout time," she said with her hands on her hips as he approached.

"Sorry." He pointed at the empty spaces that had been occupied by large tents only moments ago. "I couldn't find you."

"I know. I was supposed to be over there." She pointed toward a spacious corner across the street. "But at the last second they shoved me between Giovanni's and Patsy's."

"That's too bad," Dr. Bright rejoined.

"Oh, it's okay," Sharon replied impassively. "If people are looking for yoga, they'll find it. Hey, can you come over here for a second, Doctor?" She pointed to a box she'd been filling with leftover swag.

"Of course," he walked under the tent and stood beside her, "but please call me Duncan."

"Duncan," she took off her sunglasses and looked up at him with the afternoon light in her pretty green eyes. "That's a cool name. Is it Irish?"

"Yes," he replied.

Sharon reached into the box and pulled out a water bottle with BREATHE printed on it. "Do you want one of these?"

"Well, sure," he replied. "If you have enough."

She waved her hand over the small mountain of flasks, "Oh, I'm pretty sure I have enough."

After packing up her merchandise, Sharon invited Dr. Bright to have a smoothie with her at the Jamba Juice down the street. "Come on," she said, pulling out a buy-one-get-one-free coupon. "It's on me."

"I'd love to, but what about the rest of your stuff?" He pointed at the box.

"It's okay." She dismissed the container with a wave of her hand. "If someone wants to steal it they can."

As they sat down at a table by the window with their smoothies, two policemen outside removed the wooden barriers that had blocked off the venue and vehicles began moving down the street again.

"It happens quickly, doesn't it?" Sharon asked reflectively.

"You mean the traffic?" he inquired.

"No, I mean everything."

Although her reply was cryptic, the tone of her voice suggested she was talking about the passage of time.

"Yes," Dr. Bright replied. "It does."

"I used to bring Zander here after his soccer games." She looked wistfully at the tables and chairs. "Christ! That was three years ago, and it seems like last week."

Dr. Bright saw that the memory made her sad, so he shared a story to comfort her. "See Jimmy Fongs?" He pointed to a Chinese restaurant across the street. "I used to watch Yankees games with my daughter there."

"Wait." Sharon held up both of her hands. "You went to a Chinese restaurant to watch baseball?"

"Yep." He sipped his smoothie. "Jimmy loves the Yankees, and he's got two big-screen TVs."

"Okay," she started laughing, "that's so random."

"Why?" Dr. Bright swung an imaginary bat. "Jimmy's a big fan."

"Get out of here!" She waved him away like a fly.

"Come on, I'll show you," he said, standing up and completely forgetting about the brief, cordial visit he had planned.

"Wait." Sharon looked around at the other customers then up at him. "Where are you going?"

"To Jimmy's." He picked up his smoothie and his new water bottle. "You hungry?"

She tilted her Mighty Mango. "But we can't walk in with these."

"Of course we can," Dr. Bright exclaimed while raising his Razzmatazz. "Let's go."

From the outside, Jimmy Fongs looked like a traditional Chinese restaurant with exotic calligraphy on a neon sign and menus plastered all over the windows. However, the inside was anything but conventional—lanterns, scrolls, and inlaid tables were brutally mixed with World Series banners, the jerseys of retired Yankees, two plasma TVs, and a gigantic poster of Babe Ruth.

"This is unbelievable," Sharon said while looking around at the incongruent décor.

"Wait until you see Jimmy," and as these words left Dr. Bright's mouth, a small man in a soiled apron carrying two trays burst through the kitchen door, and with his eyes glued to the television he rapidly delivered dinners to a tableful of customers. Then, as he was heading back into the kitchen, he caught sight of the couple.

"Hey, Paul O'Neill!" he shouted and walked over.

"Paul O'Neill?" Sharon whispered.

"I'll tell you later," Dr. Bright whispered back.

"How my friend?" Jimmy grabbed and rapidly shook one of the doctor's hands.

"I'm good, I'm good," replied Dr. Bright.

"This wife?" Jimmy pointed at Sharon.

"No, no, she…"

"She girlfriend!" the chef joyfully exclaimed and slapped Dr. Bright on the back. "Girlfriend good. Wife no good." He pointed at the kitchen door and his face darkened. "Always bossy. Too bossy."

Dr. Bright laughed and looked up at the game. "What's the score?"

"Yankee have two. Oriole has four. Bottom six."

"Ouch," the doctor exclaimed.

"Nobody care. Only May. Come." Jimmy led the couple to a table, handed them menus, then went back into the kitchen.

After they sat down, Sharon, while sipping her smoothie, scrutinized the details of the décor in silence, and then after a few moments she said, "So, who's Paul O'Neill?"

Dr. Bright laughed. "He used to play right field for the Yankees."

She made circles with her hand suggesting she wanted to know more.

"And he's tall and I'm tall, hence the nickname."

"I see." Sharon smiled.

Just then the muffled clatter from the kitchen became audible as Jimmy burst through the door carrying a tray of egg rolls, spareribs, and a pitcher of water. "On house, on house," he said as he placed the appetizers in the center of the table and filled their glasses. "I come back later for order."

As he was heading back into the kitchen, Jimmy paused in front of the television and saw that the Orioles had scored another run. "Only May, only May," he muttered and went through the door.

"Well," said Sharon, surveying the table, "let me get rid of these." She picked up their empty Jamba Juice cups and brought them to a garbage can by the front door. On her journey back, she and the doctor exchanged amorous glances, and when she sat down her face was flushed.

"Well," Sharon attempted to break the romantic tension by opening a menu, "should we order something?"

"Good idea," replied the doctor.

"Any suggestions?" she asked.

"Well," he glanced at the menu, "I usually get the Kung Po beef."

"Hmmm," she scanned the choices. "I think I'll get the chicken and steamed vegetables."

They closed their menus at the same time and looked around for Jimmy with the vain hope that his return might calm the strained air.

"So," Sharon ironed the creases in the tablecloth with her hand, "you used to come here with your daughter?"

"Yes," replied Dr. Bright, thankful for the opportunity to talk about something. "We used to sit over there." He pointed to a booth by the window. "That's our lucky table."

"Why is it lucky?" She sipped her water.

"We saw Aaron Boone's big hit at that table," he said, assuming every New Yorker would know what that meant.

"Oh really?" She gazed at the table with an affectionate smile and then inquired, "So who's Aaron Boone?"

"Who's Aaron Boone?" he asked incredulously. "He beat the Red Sox with a walk-off homerun in game seven of the ALCS."

"Oh right," she playfully pretended to remember. "Aaron Boone. Got it."

"Not a big baseball fan, huh?" he asked.

"No, not really. Zander is though." She watched a bead of water slide down the glass. "Or at least he used to be. I'm not sure if he cares anymore."

Just as Dr. Bright was about to say something, his phone began to chime because he had forgotten to put it on silent.

"Oh, sorry about that." He pulled the device out of his pocket. "Let me turn this off." However, when he saw Zoe's name on the screen, he got flustered. "Oh, it's my daughter," he said as his phone continued to chime.

"So answer it," Sharon urged him.

"Okay," he touched the screen, put the phone to his ear, and opened his mouth to speak.

"Take it outside," Sharon whispered loudly while gesturing towards the annoyed customers staring at them from their tables.

"Oh right." As Dr. Bright quickly stood up to leave his knee hit the table sending three frightened egg rolls to the floor. "Sorry." He bent over to pick them up.

"Go!" Sharon exclaimed and started laughing.

"Okay," he replied and headed out the door.

Dr. Bright was so discombobulated by the time he reached the sidewalk that he'd forgotten why he came outside, and it wasn't until he heard Zoe's bubbly voice that he remembered.

"Daddy? Are you okay?" she asked.

"Yes, yes, I'm fine," he replied while stepping beneath the awning of the toy store next door.

"Are you in a restaurant or something?" Zoe inquired.

"Well… I… sort of," Dr. Bright stammered.

His daughter started laughing, "You're sort of in a restaurant?"

"Yeah… I mean I was in a restaurant." He glanced down at the sidewalk. "But now I'm standing outside."

"Dad," she said with playful scorn, "are you on a date?"

When Dr. Bright looked up, a council of dolls with inquisitive eyes were staring at him through the toy store window, so he looked the other way. "Well, not really. I'm just having dinner with a friend."

"Guy-friend or girl-friend?" Zoe shot back.

"Well," he swallowed, "a girl… I mean a lady."

"My dad's on a date!" Zoe screamed, and Dr. Bright heard a burst of cheers in the background.

"Zoe, where are *you*?" he asked, perplexed by her zealous response and the accompanying clatter.

"In my dorm room," she replied exuberantly.

"Well… who's with you?"

"My friends. We've been sitting here all afternoon taking bets on whether you were on a date or not."

"Wait." He looked at the dolls in the window again. "What?"

"Hold on, Daddy." Zoe walked into another room and closed the door. "I mean it was pretty obvious. You've sounded happier lately, and then you call me on a Saturday afternoon all excited and nervous."

"Oh," he said, floored by her prescience and intuition. "I didn't realize I…"

"Wait!" Zoe cut him off. "Where is your date right now?"

"In the restaurant," he replied.

"Where are you?" she asked.

"Well," he looked around, "I'm outside."

"WHAT!?" His daughter blew up laughing. "Are you crazy? Get back in there!"

"But…"

"Bye!" She hung up.

When Dr. Bright returned, he spied their dinners steaming on the table and he saw Sharon looking up at the television with a bemused grin.

"Sorry about that." He sat down.

"Oh, it's okay," she replied. "The game has gotten interesting."

Dr. Bright looked up and saw that the Yankees had the bases loaded in the bottom of the ninth with zero outs.

"Nice," he replied and then pointed to their untouched food. "Shall we eat?"

"Sure." Sharon smiled at him and picked up her chopsticks. "So, how is your daughter?"

"Good," he answered. "She's hanging out with friends."

"Here in the city?" Sharon asked.

"No, she's a sophomore at Cal Poly."

"California?!" she burst out exuberantly.

"Yes," replied Dr. Bright. "San Luis Obispo."

"That's awesome!" Sharon exclaimed. "What's her major?"

"Kinesiology. She wants to be a physical therapist."

"You must be very proud," she said warmly.

"I am. Zoe's a great kid."

"And I think she's your good luck charm." Sharon pointed at the TV.

Dr. Bright looked up and saw that the Yankees had just hit a grand slam that ended the game. "Yes," he said. "She is my good luck charm."

They talked about California, college, childhood dreams, and cool things to do in New York City. Dr. Bright marveled at how easy it was to talk to her—different topics arose then subtly changed like the afternoon light, and the pauses strewn throughout their conversation were organic and comfortable. A clatter from the kitchen broke the tranquility, and looking around, the couple realized that they were the only ones in the restaurant.

"I think they might be closing," Sharon said as she scanned the empty tables.

"I think you're right." Dr. Bright looked at his watch and saw that four hours had passed.

"Well," she suppressed a yawn with her hand, "should we let Jimmy and his wife go home?"

"Yes," he replied and reached for the bill tucked inside the little book on their table.

"I got this," Sharon gently brushed his hand away.

"How come?" Dr. Bright protested.

"Well, first *I* invited *you*," she withdrew some cash from her purse and placed it inside the book, "and second, this is to thank you for taking Zander in while I was in the hospital." She stood up and glanced at the kitchen door. "Should we say goodnight to Jimmy?"

"No," Dr. Bright replied. "We're set."

A pale moon wandered across the sky like a lost balloon as the lovestruck tandem walked toward Sharon's apartment in comfortable silence. When they reached her stoop, she reached inside and pulled out Dr. Bright's water bottle.

"Almost forgot to give you this." She handed it to him.

"Thank you," he said.

"And here." Sharon handed him a yoga schedule. "We have morning, afternoon, and evening classes Monday through Saturday."

"Oh cool." Dr. Bright had again forgotten his vow to try yoga.

"And take these, too." She handed him three passes to her yoga studio. "These get you in for free."

"This is very kind of you, Sharon," he said while taking a cursory glance at the papers. "Thank you."

She took one step up the stairs and faced him in the moonlight. "You're welcome, Duncan." Sharon kissed him on the cheek and turned to leave, but he gently pulled her into a passionate kiss. When their lips parted, she studied his face for a moment with moist eyes. Then, she turned, jogged up the stairs, and went inside. Walking home, Dr. Bright felt as light as the leaves stirring in the breeze, and it occurred to him that for the first time in years he felt genuinely and deeply happy.

11

On Monday, Dr. Bright finally decided to use the gym he'd been paying for since January. He had deliberately picked one next to his office for convenience, but complacency had conquered his plan and he had only gone twice. However, Sharon's toned body had made him reflect on his own neglected physique, so he had decided to get back into shape. When he got on the treadmill, he realized he had forgotten his headphones, which meant he'd have to endure his first workout without music. Fortunately, there were muted TVs he could watch while the minutes crawled by. After a slew of obnoxious commercials, the images of Central Park Lake he had seen earlier in the week filled the screens around him. Subsequently, the police chief's talking face suggested that an arrest had been made, and the doctor was anticipating the mugshots of deranged gang members to dominate the broadcast. However, when Zander's and Dawn's faces appeared on the TV in front of him, he took a wrong step and nearly fell off the treadmill. After pressing stop, he leaned closer to the silent screen in a vain attempt to listen then ran outside to buy a paper, and when he saw the headline, "Baby-Faced Butchers," with his teenage-clients' faces beneath it, his heart felt like a smashed vase.

When Dr. Bright got home, he began reading the paper. Allegedly, the two teens had "tried to bore a hole through Miller's stomach so he wouldn't be recognized." Then, they had "dumped what was left of his body into Central Park Lake." After a futile attempt to wash the blood off their clothes, they threw the knife into the lake and went to Dawn's apartment. And, after telling her doorman a preposterous story about a rollerblading accident, the two went upstairs. Howard and Louisa were in Florida, so the "bloodthirsty babes" had free reign of the "opulent penthouse." Apparently, they showered together in the master bathroom then spent the night in her parents' "hand-carved, six million-dollar Baldacchino bed." The next morning, they put their bloody clothes into one of Dawn's Louis Vuitton "crocodile leather" bags that Zander was supposed to dispose of on his way home. However, he left it in the backseat of a cab, and this eventually led to their arrest. While cleaning out his car after his shift that night, the hack found the expensive bag with the bloody clothes inside it, but because he was an undocumented immigrant fearful of deportation, he didn't report it right away. However, after a few days, his conscience got the better of him and he brought it to the police. The extravagant bag and its gory contents caught the attention of the desk sergeant who immediately notified Mark Kelly, the detective in charge of the case. The blood on the clothes matched Mr. Miller's, and Dawn had forgotten about a few receipts tucked away in a remote pocket, one revealing a black folding knife purchased on eBay last February that matched the description of the weapon police divers had found in Central Park Lake. As Dr. Bright was trying to picture Zander and Dawn committing these horrendous acts, he realized he only had twenty minutes before his first client arrived and he hopped in the shower. Leaving his apartment, he caught sight of the water bottle Sharon had given him. A century had passed since he had seen her, and the kiss that had stoked the embers of love in his heart seemed remote and far away.

As Dr. Bright stepped out onto Eighty-sixth Street, a swarm of pedestrians on their way to the subway surged at him like a title wave, and he felt as if he were trapped in some disturbing Expressionist painting. When he stepped off the curb to avoid the throng, a taxi going sixty miles per hour nearly hit him, so he got back on the sidewalk and made his way through the merciless mob. At Park Avenue, the crowd thinned out, and he was able to move at a steady clip, but he began to feel dizzy and lightheaded, which he deemed the result of hunger, and he decided to buy a bagel at a kiosk on 5th Avenue. However, as soon as he ordered, he realized that he'd left his wallet at home. After apologizing to the vexed vendor, he was assailed by a sudden thirst, so he went into Central Park to find a drinking fountain, and going down curvaceous paths lined with azaleas and rhododendrons, he realized that it had been ages since he had been able to admire the glorious array of flowers that bloom in May. He kept walking and found a bed of fading tulips near the Turtle Pond, a convocation of roses by the Delacorte Theater, and it wasn't until he saw the skyline of the Upper East Side from Belvedere Castle that it occurred to him that he'd been wandering aimlessly around Central Park for an hour, that he'd missed his morning appointments, and that he was in a state of emotional shock.

When Dr. Bright got home, he took one of the Xanax he normally used for airplanes, closed the curtains, and lay down on his bed, and once the drug restored order to his riotous brain, he began plotting out a course for the day—first, he had to contact the patients he had snubbed this morning. Under normal circumstances, he could explain his scheduling error simply by being truthful, but telling people that he'd missed their appointments because his teenage clients killed someone and that he'd spent the morning stumbling around Central Park like a deranged beggar seemed like oversharing, so he decided to say that an emergency had detained him, which was close enough to the truth. Next, Dr. Bright tried calling Sharon and Louisa, but Sharon's line went straight to voicemail and the Fontaines' maid said they weren't accepting any calls.

By the next morning, Zander and Dawn were the subject of conversation on subways, buses, and the backseats of cabs. Even Brenda Fixx, the self-absorbed owner of the sunglasses store, had an opinion about the killers.

"I heard that little bitch had her own chauffeur, and that her parents sent her to Europe anytime she wanted to go," she said disdainfully.

"And what does that prove, Brenda?" Dr. Bright inquired.

"What does that prove?" she erupted. "It proves she's a spoiled little bitch! That's what that proves!"

"Okay, so her parents gave her things. Does that automatically mean she was well taken care of and happy?" Dr. Bright parried.

"Well, she should've been, the little bitch." She raised one of her perfectly penciled-in eyebrows. "I've never been to Europe!"

And Brad, the Wall Street millionaire, normally preoccupied with his penis, had become a public avenger.

"Doctor, did you know the guy was still alive when they slit his jugular vein?"

"No, I didn't, Brad," Dr. Bright said, wishing they could talk about missing erections again.

"Fucking bastards. I hope they fry."

Evelyn, the lawyer who invented men, seemed to be the only person in Manhattan whose sentiments mirrored Dr. Bright's. Granted this murder was excessively violent, almost transcending the scope of imagination, but there hadn't even been a trial. Yet, according to the papers, and to the millions mesmerized by the power of the media, Zander and Dawn were already guilty. Evelyn, like Dr. Bright, couldn't forget that these two "butchers" were only fifteen years old.

"And if I hear about her expensive vacations in Europe one more time, I'm gonna break something," his client declared.

"Me too, Evelyn."

"Because you can be just as unhappy in Europe as you can be here. My parents sent me to England every summer and I hated it, because I knew they were just getting rid of me."

"I didn't know that, Evelyn," Dr. Bright said.

"Oh, yeah. There was an expensive fat farm there." She forced a smile.

"But aren't there plenty of those places right around here?" he asked.

"Yes, but I kept running away from those places." Evelyn looked out the window.

"You mean running home?" Dr. Bright asked softly.

"Yup, so my father decided to send me to a place I couldn't get home from."

"You never told me this before, Evelyn."

"I didn't think it mattered."

Dr. Bright thought to himself that sometimes the things closest to us are the hardest to see. Like how words become unreadable if a page is held too close to your face. The same is true with emotional issues. Those we've gotten some distance from are distinct, but when the issues are wrapped around us, they are often very difficult to see.

"Evelyn, how old were you when they first sent you away?" Dr. Bright inquired.

"Ten," she replied.

"That's awfully young."

"Yeah, but you should've seen me, Doctor." She filled her cheeks with air.

"Okay but… did your parents have issues with their weight?" he asked delicately.

She dug into her purse and pulled a picture out of her wallet. "Here," she said, handing it to him.

There were two people standing next to a boat. The guy looked like Paul Newman and the lady a young Liz Taylor.

"You'd never know I was their daughter, huh?" she asked.

"Evelyn…" He wondered how to phrase this. "How old were you when…"

"When I started getting fat? Around nine. Here." She pulled out another picture and handed it to him. It was the spitting image of her mother. And, like Liz Taylor at that age, Evelyn looked more like a beautiful woman with small features than a beautiful little girl. "Pretty, huh, Doc? I'm eight there."

"Well, yes, and you look…"

"Just like Liz Taylor, I know. Now look at this one." She handed Dr. Bright another picture. "I'm twelve in this one." The sad eyes staring at him from the bloated face were difficult to bear, so he handed back the pictures and she put them in her purse.

"For some reason, I just started binge-eating," Evelyn said impassively.

"When you were nine?" Dr. Bright inquired.

"Yup, and I started hiding food," she responded.

"Where did you hide it?" he asked.

"Oh, lots of places." Her eyes drifted around the office. "In my backpack, under my bed, in my drawers, beneath my pillows, everywhere."

The doctor thought about this and asked, "Do you remember *why* you hid it?"

"Nope," she replied. "We had plenty of money and there was plenty of food." She began to laugh. "Hey, look at this!" She pulled a squished Hershey's bar out of her purse. "Guess I'm still doing it."

"Evelyn," Dr. Bright began, "lots of people carry a snack…"

"This isn't a snack, doctor," she began unwrapping the chocolate, "this is love."

When Evelyn left, he realized this had been the first time in hours that he hadn't been consumed by thoughts of Zander and Dawn. But as soon as that idea blossomed, their faces swarmed around his mind like vultures and tore at his conscience with questions—could he have done more to halt their toxic relationship? Had he done everything in his power to keep people safe? If he had made a police report when Dawn threatened Louisa with a knife last fall, would Mickey Miller still be alive?

❧

Due to the hideously violent nature of the crime, and because Dawn was from a wealthy family, the story instantly became front page property of the New York media. It was impossible for these parents to deal with the tragedy in private. Everywhere Louisa and Howard went, someone was snapping a picture of them. Every time Sharon left her house, someone assaulted her with a microphone.

However, because Sharon wasn't a society queen like Louisa, she was no longer prey for the bloodthirsty press after a couple of weeks. In fact, if one wasn't personally connected to the story, he or she might have forgotten that a kid named Zander was involved at all. After the initial shock value had worn off, the press needed a new angle to ensure the public remained obsessed. Because the story of a middle-class boy with divorced parents was old hat, they hovered like scavengers over Dawn, "the cherub-faced brat with the heart of a rabid dog."

Articles like "Poor Little Bitch Girl" and "Deadly Debutante" were often accompanied by pictures of her in her private school uniform. Yet, the most popular picture of Dawn was the one of her sticking out her tongue at photographers the night she was arrested. Zander, now simply called "the boyfriend," merely became a reference in the media's spurious version of the story which had become gospel since neither suspect had ever given an accurate account of what happened that night.

As one blood-soaked week continued to drip into the next, the "teenage lovers," as they were now being billed, began to blame each other. This produced a fresh angle for journalists: "Romeo and Juvenile" and "East Side Story" were headlines that sprouted like weeds. "'Gut him. He's a fatty, he'll sink,'" Dawn had allegedly said, while the "boyfriend, driven by a jealous rage, had eviscerated the victim." After banishing the vision of his adolescent clients committing this horrific crime, Dr. Bright began reading another article, this one buried in the bowels of *The Post,* about Angel Valdez, the lieutenant in the Latin

Kings, once a suspect in the murder of Michael Miller. Apparently, he had been cleared of any connection to the Central Park Slaying but had recently been indicted for the murder of Tiny Lopez, the drug dealer who had been found in the dumpster. Ironically, as the doctor was considering the brutal slayings that had put New York City on edge, he got a phone call from Detective Kelly.

"Yes, Detective, I remember you, but I can't talk right now because I'm booked with clients all morning," the psychologist said, not exactly telling the truth.

"Well, could ja stop down at the station when you're through?" the cop asked.

The thought of going down to the police station depressed Dr. Bright. "Could you come here instead, Detective?"

"What's a good time for you, Doc?"

Dr. Bright looked through his appointment book. "How's two o'clock?"

After writing down the doctor's address, Detective Kelly said, "Two's fine. See ya then."

Detective Kelly had let himself into the office while Dr. Bright was wrapping up with his last client. And when the doctor saw him, he could tell that the detective had been sitting there for a while. His fedora was on the coffee table, and he was frowning at a magazine that was open on his lap. After exchanging platitudes, they walked into the office and the detective clumsily tied his motive for coming to the tail of a dwindling laugh.

"Ya know, Doc," he said, a thin smile stitched into his face. "I really gotta hand it to ya for treating that fucking nut job."

"Nut job?" the doctor asked while inviting the detective to sit with a wave of his hand.

"Dawn, the girl, that fucking psychopath. Ya know, in all my years of police work, I don't think I've ever seen anybody that twisted."

"What do you mean?" Dr. Bright settled into his chair.

"Jesus, Doc. You, of all people, should know what I mean!" Kelly cried incredulously.

"But I really don't know what you mean, Detective," the doctor responded.

Detective Kelly squinted at Dr. Bright then slowly sat down. "Look, Doc, she's caught. It's no use trying to protect her."

The implication that he was trying to shield Dawn with deception stunned him, and he asked defensively, "How am I protecting her, Detective?"

"By pretending you don't know what an evil little bitch she is."

"But I don't know that," the doctor said indignantly.

"You don't, huh?" Kelly opened his briefcase and pulled out a folder. "Then let me show ya something."

"What's that?"

"Here, see for yourself, Doc." The detective spread a pile of pictures out on the desk and pushed one at Dr. Bright. It was the image of what looked like a soggy hamburger bun floating in water.

"What the hell is that, Detective?" the doctor asked.

"It's Mr. Miller's hand."

Upon closer inspection, Dr. Bright saw that it was a hand. But, because it was drained of blood and the fingers were partially submerged, it looked like bloated bread.

"But the papers said it was nearly severed," the doctor said, with a tone of slight disbelief.

"One of them was," Kelly replied. "That's the other one."

Dr. Bright looked at it more closely, then put it down. He lowered his eyes to the floor and sighed quietly.

"And, Doc, did you know the guy was still alive when they did that?"

With heavy eyes, Dr. Bright looked back up at the detective. "No, I didn't."

"Yup, they must've thought he was dead, but when they threw him in the water he started moaning, so they fished him out. That's when they stabbed him fifty times in the chest… and those were the wounds that actually killed him. But, Doc, ya gotta see this one." He slid another picture across the desk.

"No, I think I've seen enough," the doctor objected.

"Come on, just one more," the detective insisted.

At first glance, it looked like a picture of a half-deflated parade float lying on the ground. But, when Dr. Bright held it towards the window, the picture became grotesquely clear. It was the mutilated body of a man, and it was only possible to tell where the victim's chest ended and his stomach began by the t-shirt that was half torn from his body. Various organs swam like fish out of gaping wounds. One nipple had been sliced right off. The other nipple looked like a chewed piece of pepperoni. The man's throat was slashed so many times it barely held his head in place. His face was an intricate mass of wounds. The lacerations in his cheeks were so deep the skin folded over, and one of his eye sockets had a mysterious yellow balloon coming out of it. His teeth looked like long yellow piano keys because his lips were missing. And the bushy black hair framing this hideous mess was almost more grotesque than anything, because it was the only recognizable feature that brought back the reality that this had once been a face.

"We found his lower lip in the Lake," the detective said. "The fish musta eaten the other one."

Without warning, Dr. Bright bent over and threw up in the trash can.

"I did the same thing when I saw the guy, Doc." Detective Kelly collected the pictures. "First time in fifteen years I lost it at a crime scene. Lotta guys puked that night."

Dr. Bright wiped his mouth with the back of his shaky arm, and with watery eyes muttered, "You guys…" he paused "… don't usually see stuff like that?"

"Like that?!" Kelly exclaimed. "I've never seen anything like that before in my life. And it's a good thing the little bitch left that receipt in her bag, or we woulda never thought it was kids."

"Detective, do you think we could call her Dawn?"

"Sure, Doc. So by trying to hide her crime, *Dawn*," he said, stressing her name with contempt, "got herself caught. Ironic, huh? After that, everything pretty much fell into place, because the doorman of her building not only told us what time they got to her apartment that night, he also told us they were covered in blood."

Dr. Bright was irritated by the grim pleasure the detective seemed to be getting out of telling him this. Here he was talking about irony, like they were discussing a Broadway play, when a man had been brutally murdered, and two children could feasibly spend the rest of their lives in prison. Equally as irritating was the way Detective Kelly imparted tidbits of information slowly, like a kid who hoarded Halloween candy, then gave friends bruised apples after all his good stuff was gone. The detective seemed to take special delight in recounting Dawn's "stupid rollerblading story." Apparently, she told her doorman they'd "fallen." Of course, that was to account for the blood on their clothes, though neither kid had any cuts, bruises, or rollerblades.

Dr. Bright noticed that Detective Kelly grew more and more animated when discussing Dawn's participation. It was almost like the detective had forgotten that another suspect was involved. It seemed that every time Dr. Bright mentioned Zander, the detective just clammed up, as if he'd said too much already. Yet, after the doctor asked how Louisa had been holding up, he realized that the detective's focus on Dawn had been carefully planned to elicit a response from him.

"Mrs. Fontaine? She's a disaster. I guess she's petrified of her daughter. Can't hardly blame her though. Girl's a fucking psycho, and that's why I'm having a hard time believing ya, Doc."

"A hard time believing me about what?" Dr. Bright asked.

"That you don't know what a fucked up and dangerous girl she is. I mean, she tried to attack her mother with a butcher knife last fall. You must have known about that, Doc," Kelly said reproachfully.

The vultures of guilt tore at the doctor's conscience again as he recalled Dawn's first glimpse of violence, and his own culpability in the murder bloomed in his mind.

"Yes," Dr. Bright began, "but I didn't know whether to believe..."

"Well, I guess ya know now." Kelly waved the pictures at him.

"But those don't prove..."

"They don't?" The detective put the pictures in his briefcase. "Wake up, Doc." Then, he quickly changed his tune. "Ya know, Doc, our jobs are a lot alike. I mean, we both have people telling us stories all day, and over the years, I've learned something."

"What have you learned, Detective?" Dr. Bright asked.

"People only tell us what they want us to know. See, Dawn might've acted a certain way around you because... I don't know. Maybe she needed an ally or something.

But you can't really get to know someone in a controlled setting like this office."

"So, how do you get to know someone, Detective?" Dr. Bright said, feeling patronized and insulted.

"Talk to their friends, their family. Try to see them the way others do. The best way to see them is when they can't see you." He looked at the floor like a mysterious manuscript was down there.

"Well, how do you do that, Detective?"

"Hey Doc," Kelly said, looking up. "How would you like to see the real Dawn?"

"What do you mean?"

"What are ya doing right now?" The detective stood up.

"Well, I have a few clients this afternoon…" Dr. Bright replied.

"How about tomorrow? What are you doing tomorrow?"

"Well, I have clients tomorrow, too…" he said.

Kelly pressed. "What time? When do you start?"

"Well…" Dr. Bright looked through his appointment book. "My first appointment is at ten."

"Great! Meet me at The Tombs at eight-thirty." Detective Kelly walked out the door with his briefcase.

Dr. Bright felt humiliated after the detective left because he had prided himself on knowing his clients, and he was beginning to feel as if he hadn't understood Dawn at all. All Kelly had to do was lay out a few pictures and point out a few details and the doctor's confidence had collapsed. Adding insult to injury, the crude cop was now offering to give Dr. Bright lessons in analysis, which was mortifying, but he felt compelled to accept the detective's invitation because if the heart of a killer had been beating inside Dawn all along, he needed to know.

∽

The next morning, Dr. Bright took a cab to "The Tombs," the colloquial name for the Manhattan Detention Complex in Lower Manhattan that houses criminals awaiting trial.

Detective Kelly led the doctor into a room with a big black window and closed the door. Five seconds later, the window snapped bright and a room with a table and chairs appeared on the other side. A heavyset man walked in with a female officer, followed by Dawn in a bright orange jumpsuit. With the makeup washed off her face, she looked like she was twelve years old.

"Poor kid," Dr. Bright said.

"Kid huh?" Detective Kelly laughed. "Oh yeah," he said, flipping a switch. "I forgot to do that."

Suddenly, through a speaker, Dr. Bright heard the female officer say, "Do you want me to stay, Sergeant?"

"No, I can handle it." The sergeant's voice sounded like a concrete mixer.

"You be good now, Dawn," cautioned the officer.

Without looking up, Dawn gave her the finger and the woman left with a scowl.

"So," said the sergeant, as he looked through his papers, "gonna cooperate today?"

"Got a cigarette for me, baby?" Dawn's voice was an octave higher than usual. "I'll give ya a blow job."

"No thanks," he said disdainfully.

"I'll even swallow it like a good little girl," she said, batting her lashes at him.

"Well, we're already off to a bad start." He tossed his pencil down.

"Yeah, but you know you're turned on, Sergeant." She leaned forward. "Stand up so I can see your big erection."

The sergeant just shook his head in disgust and Dawn started laughing. "That proves it! That proves it! If you weren't hard, you'd stand up!"

Detective Kelly turned the sound down. "There's your 'poor kid,' Doc. Is that the Dawn you know?"

"No," said Dr. Bright, befuddled by Dawn's behavior.

"Has she ever offered you a blow job?"

"Of course not!" Dr. Bright protested.

"Would ya tell me if she did, Doc?"

Deeply offended, Dr. Bright just stared at the detective with porcelain eyes.

After a tense moment, Kelly said, "Look, Doc, for what it's worth, I believe ya."

Through the window, Dawn was blowing kisses at the crimson sergeant.

"I've seen it a billion times," the detective continued. "People come down here to the station thinking their kids couldn't have possibly committed a crime…"

"Then you bring them to the magic window and show them how wrong they were. Right, Detective?" Dr. Bright inquired bitterly.

"Nope. You're the first guy I've ever done this for," Kelly replied, seemingly unaware of the doctor's acerbity.

"Well, I'm honored," the doctor retorted.

"I didn't do it to honor you, Doc."

Dawn was taunting the sergeant by raising her shirt with her handcuffed hands.

"And I'm not showing ya this stuff to make ya feel bad, either," the detective continued.

"Then, why are we here?" Dr. Bright looked at the detective because he couldn't look at Dawn anymore.

"I need your help, Doc."

"*You* need *my* help?" the doctor said, with palpable sarcasm.

"Hey, look, Doc, the same kinda shit has happened to me. You think you're gettin' through to someone, then they prove you wrong. It's part a' the job."

Doctor Bright looked at Dawn again and she now seemed to be conversing normally with the sergeant.

"So, Doc, will ya help us?" Detective Kelly asked.

"How?" the doctor asked.

"Well, we're still tryin' ta find out exactly what happened the night of the murder, and we can't get a straight story. He's blaming her an' she's blaming him an'… I was thinking maybe you could get the truth out of them."

Dawn stared at the wall with sad eyes, as though she knew Dr. Bright was there.

"So, Doc, will ya help us?" Detective Kelly asked.

"Wait a minute." The doctor turned away from the window. "You want me to help you convict my own clients?"

"Not exactly." The detective placed a hand on Dr. Bright's shoulder and led him into the hall. "See, right now they're both facin' twenty-five to life without parole, but if it turned out that *one of them* stabbed the guy," he jabbed his thumb toward the wall where Dawn was, "while the other kid only watched, it might go easier on one of 'em."

"So, you think Dawn did it, Detective?" Dr. Bright asked.

"I'm not sure," the cop replied. "But I don't see why both should rot in jail for something only one of 'em did."

Riding in the elevator, Dr. Bright realized he was at a crossroad of his conscience—ethically, he was supposed to safeguard the welfare and rights of his clients, and helping police convict one of them didn't seem to fit with those principles. But both were already facing life sentences, so his assistance at this point couldn't hurt, he reasoned. Outside the station, he saw a handcuffed teenager in an orange jumpsuit being escorted by three mammoth cops to a van parked by the curb—the kid's eyes were glued to the ground like tarnished pennies, and he emitted a sense of heartbreaking hopelessness. Within seconds, the guards packed him inside, slammed the doors, and headed off to some forsaken destination, and there on the station steps, Dr. Bright made his decision to help police sort out the mystery of that gruesome night. If it turned out that he could spare one of his clients from a lifetime in prison, he had to do it.

⌘

Although he only had fifteen minutes to get from lower Manhattan to his office on the Upper East Side for his appointment with Stan, the former financial advisor. Dr. Bright miraculously made it on time. His client had lost ten pounds since he began therapy four months ago, and the dark circles under his eyes along with his tepid complexion suggested he'd started to use cocaine again. However, he was in such an agitated state that Dr. Bright had refrained from broaching the subject. Additionally, Stan had become obsessed with the "Baby-Faced Butchers," and his knowledge of the case gleaned from the tabloid articles he had read formed the bitter invectives that dominated their conversations.

"Now that stupid Dawn bitch is saying they found the guy unconscious and tried to revive him. And just two days ago, she said her boyfriend went psycho with jealousy and stabbed the guy." Stan was gripping the arms of his chair so tightly, Dr. Bright was afraid they were going to break. "Imagine her changing her story like that. I mean you'd have to be a fucking fool to believe anything that little cunt said. Tried to revive the guy?! How fucking ridiculous is that?!"

"Cut the crap, Stan!" Dr. Bright suddenly scolded him. "We're wasting our time talking about those kids. Now, when did you start using cocaine again?" As these words left the doctor's mouth, he realized that the tollbooth between what he believed and what he said had malfunctioned, and now his thoughts had filled the room with a foul-smelling tension. It was as if Stan's batteries had suddenly died. For thirty seconds or so, he just sat there and stared at the floor, while his face grew more and more pale. Then, just as quickly, he lit up like a jukebox, flew across the room, and punched Dr. Bright in the face.

Thankfully, the doctor's chair had wheels, so he didn't have to absorb the full blow. But, after the chair's brief journey, his head snapped back and hit the wall, which was equally unpleasant. On the bright side, however, the chair hit the wall so hard that it stood the doctor up, so he was able to avoid Stan as he proceeded to fly at him again. When Stan turned to make another charge, Dr. Bright grabbed the brass lamp that had been knocked over during the fray. He gave his furious client the choice of leaving or getting smacked. Fortunately, Stan chose to walk out, and Dr. Bright didn't have to brain him.

Remembering his failure to inform authorities about Dawn's domestic violence months ago and the ramifications of his negligence, Dr. Bright instantly went down to the Seventeenth Precinct and filed a report about the incident with Stan. However, when he made it clear that he wasn't pressing charges, the visibly irritated desk sergeant told the doctor that chasing after petty offenders without the victim's cooperation was a "big waste of time." And walking up Lexington Avenue an hour later after several botched attempts to catch a cab, Dr. Bright realized the sergeant was right.

When he got back to his office, a crimson bruise was already spreading beneath his left eye and the back of his head which had hit the wall during the fray was throbbing. After taking two Advil, he reclined his chair and closed his eyes in search of a much-needed nap, but a disturbing parade of images prevented sleep from happening—gigantic effigies of Zander and Dawn drifted by with gigantic knives as a deflated Mickey Miller with a million gashes flailed helplessly at their feet; after these specters passed, a throng of policemen in the distance slowly approached followed by a shackled prisoner, and when the procession got closer, Dr. Bright saw himself shuffling behind the crowd of cops. For some reason when he opened his eyes, he had a desperate urge to call Sharon, but because he'd already left three messages that weren't returned, he decided against it.

ℰ℘

A week later, on a bus en route to a neighborhood formally known as Five Points, Dr. Bright saw the newspaper headline, "Dawn's Diary," clutched between the fingers of the person sitting next to him. Without reservation, he leaned over and scanned the article in his neighbor's paper. From what he could read, it appeared that investigators had uncovered a journal of Dawn's from two years ago that "shed light on the homicidal mind of a very deranged girl." The article went on to say that this would certainly prove to be a "very damning piece of evidence" when the case came to trial. Investigators couldn't comment specifically on any of these "chilling revelations." But they promised jurors would be "shaken," especially by the poems displaying Dawn's "unflagging enmity for mankind."

As he sat back in his seat, Dr. Bright was bothered by a few things he had just read. First of all, if the investigators couldn't discuss these "chilling revelations," why bring them up in the first place? Clearly, it was just another ploy to sell papers, using the lives of ruined people as the dangling carrots. The other irksome quality was the "damning piece of evidence" in question. Anyone who's ever read, or remembers writing, teenage poetry knows what maudlin, misanthropic, and melodramatic crap it is. And as he entered The Tombs, Dr. Bright thought, if adolescent diaries are now being used as "damning evidence," then 95 percent of the teenagers in this world are "homicidal."

"Who do ya wanna see first, Doc?" Detective Kelly asked.

Dr. Bright thought about it. "Either one is fine."

The cop glanced down at his watch. "Well, you might wanna try Zander, 'cause Dawn's not having such a good morning. She attacked a guard at breakfast and when they were restraining her, she hit her head."

"Is she all right?!" the doctor asked emphatically.

"Yeah, yeah, just a bump," Kelly replied. "She's in the infirmary now, so why don't we get ya up to see Zander?"

"Wait a minute, Detective. Have Dawn's parents been notified?"

"Doc," the cop laughed. "If we notified Dawn's parents about every incident, we'd have to have 'em on speed dial. Besides, it's only a bump, so..."

"I don't care if it's only a bump," Dr. Bright interrupted him. "She's hurt and they ought to be told."

"Yeah? Then here." Kelly pulled out his phone. "You call 'em."

Detective Kelly punched a few buttons then handed the phone to Dr. Bright. After perhaps twenty-three beeps, Louisa's voice emerged. "You've reached Louisa and Howard. We're not home right now, but if you leave your name, phone number, and the time you called, we'll get back to you"… *BEEP.*

"Hi Louisa and Howard, this is Dr. Bright," he spoke into the device. "I'm down at the police station and Dawn has been injured. Please either give me or Detective Kelly a call when you get this message. Thanks."

Dr. Bright handed back the phone, feeling triumphant. "Don't like to call them, Detective?"

"No, that's not it, Doc. I just don't see the point in leaving another message. Those beeps you heard before the machine picked up? More than half of them are from me."

"And they won't call you back?" the doctor asked.

Kelly put his phone in his pocket and said, "They're out of the country."

"Out of the country?! Where did they go?" Dr. Bright exclaimed.

"Well," the detective replied, "Mr. Fontaine's secretary pretended not to know their exact whereabouts, but I did a little digging and found out they got a place on the French Riviera."

"Wait," Dr. Bright tried to digest the information. "Their daughter's been charged with murder and they fly off to the Riviera? Isn't there a law against that, Detective?"

"You've got a romanticized view of things, Doc," Kelly said bitterly.

Surprised by the detective's bitterness, the doctor asked, "How am I being romantic?"

"Because parents do this kinda crap all the time. Do you know how many abandoned kids there are in this fucking city, Doc?"

"No, well," the doctor stammered, "do you mean like the kids living in halfway houses and foster care?"

"Foster care?" The Detective guffawed. "Those are the kids Social Services knows about." Then, he turned his back and walked away, and Dr. Bright followed him.

Zander was in a part of The Tombs the cops called the "Bates Motel." "Bates" stood for the psychopaths it housed, and "Motel" meant it wasn't their permanent home. This place was a holding tank for criminals with pending trials. Detective Kelly pointed at a cell and left, and Dr. Bright saw Zander lying on a cot facing the wall. When the doctor first spoke, the boy didn't move, and when he finally turned around his eyes were flooded with despair. Dr. Bright explained that he'd been trying to get in touch with Sharon, and Zander said in a rusty voice that she wasn't doing very well. The teen said she came every day during visitors' hours and "blubbered." But his sad face belied his harsh words, and Dr. Bright knew the boy was sickened about the ordeal's impact on his mother. When asked if his father had visited, Zander's eyes crashed to the floor and Dr. Bright took that as a "no."

During a lull in their conversation, the entire cell block seemed to be engulfed by an almost hostile stillness. Dr. Bright realized that this would be the worst thing about incarceration—silence, the soil of thoughts, where past deeds blossom into grotesque flowers of guilt and regret.

"Have you seen her yet, Doc?" Zander's voice startled him.

"Dawn? No, not yet. I was planning on seeing her after you."

The boy sat up abruptly as if a cruel puppeteer had yanked hard on his strings. "Be careful, man."

"Why should I be careful?" the doctor asked.

"Because she's a fuckin' twisted, psychopathic bitch, that's why." Zander stamped his feet like he was testing the strength of the floor. "Fuckin' bitch went totally crazy on me."

"What do you mean?"

A closing door shattered Dr. Bright's question and Detective Kelly appeared holding two Styrofoam cups of coffee. "So, how's everything going?"

"Fine, Detective. Is my time up or something?"

"No, Doc," he said handing him one of the cups. "Just wanted to see how everything was going."

"Everything's fine," said Dr. Bright, hoping his furtive frown would get the detective to leave.

"Oh, I see." Kelly spun around and walked away. "Come see me when you're through."

Zander had already fallen back into his prone position on the cot facing the wall, obviously letting the doctor know *they* were through.

"Tampon Bay," as Detective Kelly referred to it, was a cell block much like the Bates Motel with one obvious difference: it was painted a disturbing shade of pink, reminiscent of sunburned skin. Dr. Bright didn't recall seeing many prisoners in Bates Motel, but Tampon Bay was brimming with them. The color in the prisoners' fingers was gone from gripping the bars so tightly, and at first glance it looked like a gallery of dead hands.

As Dr. Bright moved down the hall, he noticed the prisoners' eyes. Some of the eyes were frightened. Others were forest fires burning him down with their furious glances. The woman in the cell next to Dawn's had long, black hair and starving eyes. She looked like one of those sirens who had lured sailors to their deaths back in Homer's time, and when Dr. Bright approached, she grabbed the iron bars and stared at him.

"Hey Doc," said Dawn. She had an enormous gauze bandage wrapped around her skull.

"How are you feeling, Dawn?" Dr. Bright inquired.

"Not so good," she said, touching the bandage with her finger.

"What happened?" He pointed to her head.

"I don't give those dykes what they want. That's what happened."

"You mean," he caught sight of the siren next door, "they're sexually abusing you?"

"They're trying to," she replied.

The siren in the next cell traced her lips with a bright red tongue.

"Well, I'll notify Detective Kelly," Dr. Bright said.

"Don't bother, Doc. Everyone knows what goes on in here."

"I'm sure Detective Kelly doesn't know about it, Dawn."

The siren drew designs on her chest with her finger so that Dr. Bright could see the shape of her breasts beneath the orange jumpsuit.

"You know, Doc, for an intelligent guy…" Dawn let her scowl finish the rest of her sentence.

"For an intelligent guy what?" he asked.

The siren was still drawing designs, so Dr. Bright moved to the right until she disappeared from his view.

"Come on Dawn, for an intelligent guy what?"

"For an intelligent guy, you act like a fucking retard sometimes."

The siren moved closer so he could see her again.

"I mean, look at Maxine." Dawn pointed her thumb down the hall towards a guard who was watching them with granite eyes. "Can't you tell she's a fucking bull dyke?"

"Dawn, just because someone's a lesbian doesn't mean they molest children." The siren smiled at him when he said the word "lesbian."

"Well, that one fucking does!" Dawn sat up quickly, grabbed her head and lay back down.

"Jesus, Dawn, you're really hurt," he said tenderly.

"Oh no, I'm fine," she said, little tears formed on her lashes. "I'm making all this up. My head doesn't really hurt! My parents aren't really in France, and no one beat me up this morning because I wouldn't suck the head of their nightstick!"

The eavesdropping siren licked the bars of her cell with closed eyes.

Dawn continued her rant. "No one held me down my first night here and thumb-fucked me in the bathroom! No one filled my vagina with liquid soap." She was beginning to sob. "So, why don't you just go back to your little office and leave me the fuck alone!" Dawn rolled over towards the wall and the siren started rubbing her breasts against the bars of her cell.

"Dawn?" Dr. Bright said, while the siren started rubbing her crotch with one hand and both breasts with the other. "I'm going to look into all this stuff for you."

"Terrific," she said with the enthusiasm of a cancer patient in the last stages of chemotherapy.

"Because if what you're saying is true..."

"But it's not true," she cut him off. "I'm making it all up." Her voice was muffled and distant. "I mean why the fuck should I tell the truth?" She rolled over and faced him. "I've lied about everything else, right?"

The siren next door let out a moan then fell to her cot with both hands on her crotch.

"Shut up, Trista!" Dawn got up and kicked the wall that separated the two cells. "She's fucking herself, right?"

"Well," said Dr. Bright, trying not to look, "I think so."

"That's all she ever does, the fucking pig!"

The siren was now thrusting her hips at the ceiling.

Dawn sat down and started crying again. "I don't think I can take it anymore." As she wiped her nose on her sleeve, a lascivious sigh from the siren's cell attached itself to the air.

"Shut up! Shut up! Shut up!" Dawn flew off her bed and began punching the wall with her little white fists.

Suddenly, Maxine appeared out of nowhere, screaming, "Open six! Open six! Open six!"

The cell door opened, and Maxine came in and wrestled Dawn to her bed.

"My head! My head! My head!" the injured girl cried with both her arms wrapped around her bandages.

"Watch out for her head!" Dr. Bright grabbed Maxine's arm.

"Let go of me!" the guard screamed.

"Not till you let go of her!"

Suddenly, it was as if he was in a movie theatre where something had gone wrong with the projector. Everything was dark except for purple stains appearing and disappearing on the black screen. Then, two mouths appeared.

"Doc? Can ya hear me, Doc?" The first mouth flapped like laundry in a breeze.

"Let's give him a little more time," the second mouth flapped. "That was quite a blow."

"Where am I?" Dr. Bright asked while looking around at an unfamiliar room.

"The Tombs. I'm Captain Hunt. You're in my office. How do you feel?"

"What the hell am I doing here?" the doctor asked.

A face appeared. "Doc? Doc? It's me, Detective Kelly. Ya came down for Zander and Dawn, remember?"

"Oh yeah, I remember," Dr. Bright lied.

"Oh good, he remembers. Now, how many fingers do I have?" Detective Kelly held up two fingers.

"Two," said Dr. Bright, touching the top of his head. "What hit me?"

"Serena… I mean, Officer Sanchez. She's the DH on our softball team. Hit fifty homers this season."

"Fifty-one," Dr. Bright mumbled, pointing to his head.

"Was it fifty?" Captain Hunt frowned. "I thought she hit forty-something."

"Nah, fifty. I was there when she did it," Detective Kelly replied.

Their voices faded as the lost minutes of Dr. Bright's life struggled to return—someone on the floor grabbing her crotch, someone punching the wall, a river of arms, a scream like a rose about to be clipped, darkness.

"Uh, excuse me, gentlemen?" Dr. Bright interrupted. "Could one of you tell me why Officer Sanchez hit me?" he asked, somewhat regaining his composure.

"You grabbed Maxine," said Detective Kelly. "She came in to subdue Dawn and you tried to stop her… remember, Doc?"

"No."

"I guess you thought she was hurting Dawn… anyway, that's when Serena clocked you."

"Jesus." He felt his head again. "Where's Dawn now?"

"She's resting," Detective Kelly looked at Captain Hunt. "I think we should bring him to the hospital."

"The hospital?" Dr. Bright said, stumbling as he tried to stand up. "I don't need to go to the hospital." The room tilted.

"Well, Doc, can we give you a lift anywhere?"

"No, I'm fine."

"Okay, well… stop by anytime… okay, Doc?" Detective Kelly said.

"Okay." Dr. Bright stepped out of the room like he was walking through a field of tall flowers.

12

The next night, Dr. Bright went back to the police station. Even though Zander and Dawn were being held for murder, they were still his clients and perhaps he could help them. Light from Detective Kelly's office elbowed its way into the hall, and it dawned on Dr. Bright why The Tombs was so goddamned depressing—no windows. There were a few, the little ones in the stairwell, the barred one in the Bates Motel. But, for the most part, this place lived off the sickly glow of fluorescent bulbs. His hand poised to knock was restrained by the sight of Detective Kelly slumped over a map of Central Park on his desk. The cop was holding his face as if waiting for the glue on his new head to dry, and his trembling lips suggested he was speaking with someone Dr. Bright couldn't see.

"Doc, Jesus!" said Detective Kelly, sitting up suddenly.

"Sorry, Detective, I…"

"It's alright, it's alright." The detective pointed to a chair. "Have a seat."

"Any luck?" Dr. Bright said, nodding at the map.

"Nah, they're still blaming each other."

"Well, look," the doctor began, "I was wondering if I could see the kids."

"That'd be great, Doc, but Dawn's lawyer's here, and I'm not sure when she'll be through."

"Well, what about Zander?"

The detective grabbed an enormous ring of keys, "Sure. Come on."

On their way to Bates Motel, Dr. Bright mentioned Dawn's allegations of sexual abuse by the guards.

"That explains why her lawyer's here," Kelly said facetiously.

"Do you think there's any truth to what she said, Detective?"

"Truth?" the gumshoe scoffed. "From the mouth of that little psychopath? Not a chance."

After walking down a dreary hallway, they reached an enormous metal door with rivets all over it.

"Jesus!" Dr. Bright exclaimed. "This looks like the door to Dr. Frankenstein's laboratory."

"Yeah, the bitch is three inches thick," Kelly replied.

After the detective tried a few stubborn keys, one slipped in, and an ominous click filled the hallway. Then, the enormous door opened onto a long corridor with one dim window at the end.

"Doc, do you remember which cell is Zander's?"

"Not really," said Dr. Bright, startled by how much more depressing the cell block was at night.

Detective Kelly pointed down the hall. "Number six. Four cells down on your right."

"Where will you be?"

"I'll be right out here, Doc."

"Okay." Dr. Bright went to shake his hand, but the detective had already walked away.

Zander was lying in bed reading *Hot Rod*. He looked even more thin and pale than before, and when Dr. Bright asked him how he was doing, the boy cut him off.

"Fuckin' guy put a Chevy engine in a Mustang!"

"What's that, Zander?" the doctor asked.

"This fuckin' guy," the boy said, shaking his head at the magazine. "Completely restores a '66 Mustang. Gets the original seats, rugs, steering wheel. Even scours the globe for the right lighter, then puts in a Chevy engine. What a fuckhead."

Dr. Bright thought about the difference between himself at age fifteen reading *Hot Rod* in his bedroom with STP stickers all over the walls and Zander reading his in a jail cell.

The boy continued, "Fuckin' guy says the Chevy engine's quicker. Fuckin' bullshit."

"Ford engine quicker?" the doctor inquired.

"Yeah, but that ain't the point. If you think the Chevy's quicker, then restore a fuckin' Chevy. Don't go to all this trouble restoring a Mustang then put in a Chevy engine. Makes no fuckin' sense. And, I mean, the main thing you want original is the fuckin' engine. Now it ain't even a Mustang. Looks like one, but it ain't."

"Yeah, I see what you mean, Zander."

"It's like those chicks with dicks and balls," the boy interjected.

"Chicks with dicks and balls?" Dr. Bright questioned.

"Yeah, those fuckin' mutant chicks in porno flicks with big tits, dicks, and balls. Doc, whaddya call them fuckin' freaks?"

Dr. Bright thought about it for a moment and then said, "Hermaphrodites?"

"Nah." Zander looked at the doctor like he was as stupid as the guy who crossbred the Chevy and the Mustang.

Dr. Bright scanned his mind for colloquialisms. "You mean she-males, Zander?"

"That's it, Doc! She-males! Those fuckin' freaks a' nature. That's what the guy did. Made his fuckin' Mustang a she-male. Poor fuckin' car. Now it's all confused. Hey, Doc, j'ever have a she-male for a client?"

"No, Zander."

"C'mon, Doc, did ya?" He grinned mischievously at Dr. Bright.

"Really, Zander, I don't think I've ever counseled a hermaphrodite."

"There ya go with that fuckin' word again," he said, frowning. "Fuckin' guy with his big words. Don't mean shit."

The doctor considered the boy's words then said, "What do you mean, Zander?"

"Well, where do they getcha, all those big words?"

"Where do they *get me*?" Dr. Bright asked.

"Yeah, and where the fuck did they get me?! Come talk to your sorry ass once a week and what did it do?! Huh, Doc?! Tell me!" He threw his magazine and it bounced off the bars. "Where the fuck did they get me?" His head hit the pillow and he let out a sob.

"I don't blame you for being angry, Zander."

After a minute of silence, Zander spoke. "I didn't really mean what I said."

"That's okay."

"Nah, but really. There wasn't nothing you coulda done anyway… I been doin' drugs and runnin' around with a bad crowd since I was ten. You couldn'ta fixed me anyway."

"You don't need to be fixed. You're a good kid."

The boy picked up his magazine. "Good kids don't go around stabbin' people."

Dr. Bright was stunned by Zander's admission, but he knew this wasn't the time to stumble. "Good people do bad things all the time. This good/bad stuff is nonsense. We're all good and bad. We're all corruptible. Everyone."

"Well, I sure am corrupted," the teen rejoined.

"But it's not your fault, Zander. I mean look at your life—ten years old, and you were doing drugs, running around with a bad crowd. That's tragic."

"It wasn't so tragic, Doc."

"Ten-year-olds should be playing with GI Joes, not crack pipes."

Zander laughed and wiped his eyes.

"What did your parents say when you'd come home stoned?" Dr. Bright asked.

"Well, my dad wasn't around, and my mom worked late."

Here, Dr. Bright suggested that perhaps drugs had played a role in the night of the murder, and the boy grew defensive.

"Listen to me," Zander said, piercing him with his sulfurous eyes. "That ain't it! My mom's been trying to say the same shit, but it ain't true! It's like you guys are blamin' the drugs cause you can't accept the fact that drugs didn't murder the guy, I did! Me and a fuckin' psycho bitch!"

"I'm not saying the drugs committed murder. I'm saying that if you were both high, they probably played a part…"

"C'mon, Doc, take off the fuckin' blinders. What am I in here for?"

"You're in here for allegedly murdering a man," Dr. Bright whispered.

"No, Doc." Zander shook his head. "There ain't no *allegedly* about it. I'm in here for murderin' a guy."

"Look, Zander, no one's guilty until they've been proven…"

"Nothing needs to be proven because I'm fuckin' guilty!" the boy screamed. "You hear that, Detective Kelly?!" He stood up. "I'M GUILTY!"

"Zander..."

He stood up. "I CUT THE GUY'S EYES OUT! I FED HIM TO THE FISH!"

"Everything okay here?" A guard showed up.

"Yes, he's okay, Officer..." Dr. Bright looked at his nametag. "Officer Shields. He's just a little upset."

"OFFICER SHIELDS KNOWS WHO DONE IT! DONTCHA OFFICER SHIELDS!?" Zander shouted with visible venom.

"No, but I know who's going back to B Block if he don't shut up," said the guard, taking out his keys.

Zander approached the bars. "SHOVE B BLOCK UP YOUR FUCKIN ASS, PRICK!"

"Officer Shields listen to me," Dr. Bright tried to intercede, "he's just a little..."

The sound of a slamming door obliterated the rest of Dr. Bright's sentence, and Detective Kelly appeared. "Get lost, Shields."

"But, Detective," the guard sheepishly began, "he just called me a..."

"So you're gonna let a kid... come here." They slowly walked away together. The back of Detective Kelly's jacket pulled tighter and tighter with each muffled point he made, as the guard seemed to get smaller and smaller. Then, the Detective disappeared around a corner and the guard scurried down the cell block like a mouse.

"Okay, Zander, all right," said Dr. Bright, petting the air with his hands. "He's gone, so we can relax."

"Relax, relax... that's your favorite word, ain't it, Doc?"

"I just don't want you to get into any more trouble," the doctor reasoned.

"Any more trouble? I'm in fuckin' jail for murder. How much more trouble can I get in?" Zander's voice abruptly softened. "They ain't gonna keep me in here forever, ya know."

"No?" the doctor asked.

"Nah, they'll probably send me to Leavenworth or Sing Sing. One a' them fuckin' places." He started to sway from fatigue. "Yeah, Doc, that's really gonna suck when that happens."

"Well, don't give up hope, Zander. I mean, the trial hasn't even begun yet."

"Yeah." The boy suddenly sat down. "Wanna hear somethin' depressing, Doc? Tomorrow's my fuckin' birthday."

"Oh shit!" The words slipped out of Dr. Bright's mouth.

"Told ja it was depressing."

"Zander, I'm sorry… I didn't mean…"

"It's okay. No one knows better than me how depressing it is."

Dr. Bright began to say something else, but Zander waved his words away as if they were mosquitoes and lay down on his cot. "I'm gonna spend my sixteenth birthday in jail and there ain't nothin' you can do about it, Doc."

When he got back to his apartment, Dr. Bright recalled *his* sixteenth birthday—his father had driven him down to the DMV to get his driving permit, and after standing in obnoxious lines and filling out a million annoying papers, he had driven their 1968 Buick Skylark back home. Normally, the maroon coupe that his father washed and waxed every weekend would have been off limits to Duncan, but because it was a special occasion, his dad had given him the keys. He remembered the hum of the V-8 engine as he drove through the streets and feeling confident and calm, a radical departure from the feelings that had dogged him after his mother's death—since her passing, there had been a stranger living inside him, and now he had felt like his hands were his again.

Recalling the memory evoked a mixture of feelings within Dr. Bright—part of him celebrated the poignant moment in his own life, while another part grieved for Zander who would wake up on his sixteenth birthday in jail.

13

When Dr. Bright got to work the next morning, there was a message on his machine from Sharon. At first, he thought it was an electronic telemarketer because of the static, but that static was the sound of her crying.

"Doctor, this is Sharon," she sniffed. "Zander's mother. I'm sorry I haven't called you…" She sniffed again. "…but I've been busy." Here there was silence. "I just wanted to tell you what a wonderful man you are." She paused. "I just talked to Zander and you're… such a good man. He… it meant the world to him that you came. See, his father," she said, catching her breath, "he doesn't care, and I know Zander looks up to you." Saying this seemed to help her tears subside. "And I wanted to tell you I'm going there tonight around seven to bring him a few presents… and if you wanted to come he'd… we'd love to have you. Okay… goodbye."

Afternoon passed like a movie on fast forward. Shadows moved across his walls like flocks of dark geese, and before Dr. Bright had time to wonder where the day was going, it was already gone. When he arrived at The Tombs, Detective Kelly had already gone home so another officer brought him up to Bates Motel where Sharon was sitting on a chair outside Zander's cell with a pile of presents torn apart at her feet.

"Oh, Zander, look who's here." The thickness in her voice suggested recent tears. "It was so good of you to come, Doctor." She held out her hand and when their fingers touched the amorous feelings that had been dormant exploded inside him.

"Nice to see you again, Sharon," said Dr. Bright, trying to conceal his emotions. "How's it going, Zander?"

The boy rolled over and faced the wall.

"They opened his presents," Sharon whispered, "and he's…"

"He's pissed off!" Zander finished her sentence. "Mom, you don't have to whisper!" he shouted.

"Well, that's understandable," Dr. Bright said, wondering what to do with her fingers.

"Understandable?!" the teen objected. "What's my mom gonna do, bring me a fuckin' gun?"

"No, Zander, I meant it's understandable that you're pissed off."

Sharon took her fingers back.

"Fuckin' won't even let me keep my fuckin' birthday presents. Fuckin' called 'em contraband, those fuckin' bastards."

Dr. Bright looked down at the small pile of presents.

"Well, Zander," the doctor said, as Sharon looked up at him with the tears she had unsuccessfully tried to subdue running down her cheeks, "I think they'll let you keep your gifts."

"Nah, Doc." The boy faced them again. "They said they'd take 'em when she left."

Sharon nodded in agreement.

"Well, I don't think that's such a good idea, so here's what we're going to do," said Dr. Bright, opening his briefcase. "I'll take them home for tonight, and tomorrow when Detective Kelly gets here, we'll see if you can keep them."

"Thank you, Doctor," said Sharon, wiping her face.

"You're welcome." Dr. Bright took out the stack of *Hot Rods* he had bought for Zander. "Here you go, sport."

Zander started to get off the cot, but a voice knocked him back down. "Get your hands away from those bars!" An enormous cop approached.

"They're just some magazines, Officer," Dr. Bright said as he was engulfed by the cop's enormous shadow.

"It doesn't matter," the storybook giant responded. "It's against the law to smuggle in contraband."

There he stood, six foot six, with shoulders in separate zip codes, a nightstick, a can of mace, and a big black pistol. So basically, Dr. Bright thought, he could knock me down, mace my eyes, hit me with his stick, and then shoot me.

"Listen, Officer Evans," said the doctor, reading the nametag pinned on the officer's shirt, "it's the kid's birthday."

"Yeah, I gathered that. These," he said, pointing his nightstick at the pile of presents and staring through Dr. Bright with primordial eyes, "have to leave with you."

"Okay, Officer," the doctor acquiesced.

Officer Evans stared at Dr. Bright for a few more seconds, then picked up the magazines, which looked like matchbooks in his hands. "*Hot Rod,* huh?" He looked in at Zander and appeared to be visibly moved by the birthday boy in the cell. "Here kid," he said, pushing the magazines through the bars. "You can keep these."

Zander got up slowly, swayed a little, then came over and took the magazines.

"Got a name, kid?" the cop asked.

"Zander," the teen replied.

"I'm Officer Evans."

"Nice ta meet cha, Officer Evans."

Sharon and Dr. Bright were both shocked by Zander's propriety, which didn't last very long.

"Hey, Doc, should I tell Officer Evans about the she-male?"

"The what?" A smile flickered across the cop's enormous face.

"The she-male. But, Doc, what was the other name you used for them freaks? Herpes?"

"Herpes?" Sharon and Officer Evans said at the same time and looked at Dr. Bright.

"No," Dr. Bright began, "that's not the way it happened… he…"

Zander cut the doctor off. "Well, this fuckin' jackass put a Chevy engine in his Mustang…"

"Who did?" The enormous cop scowled at Dr. Bright. "You?"

"No, no, some guy in Zander's magazine," the doctor replied in a shaky voice.

"Yeah, some fuckin' dickhead out in California."

"Oh." Officer Evans decided he wouldn't eat Dr. Bright after all. "Well, what do you expect? It's California."

"Yeah, well anyway," Zander continued, "this fuck put a Chevy engine in a Mustang and the Doc here called him a she-male."

"Hey, Doc, you're okay!" Officer Evans slapped him on the shoulder, and the doctor almost stumbled.

"And Doc," Zander said, enjoying himself, "what was your other word for 'em?"

"Hermaphrodites," Dr. Bright said, giving up.

After standing around a few more minutes listening to Zander's tirade on she-males, Corvettes, and California, the huge cop, now as friendly as a tamed bear, decided he'd better get back to work. And when he left, all their happiness went with him. Because the minute he was gone, the reality of Zander being in jail on his sixteenth birthday was back. So they sat in silence, which was broken only by occasional coughs, until Sharon yawned.

"Ma, you should go," Zander said.

"Well, I…" She looked at Dr. Bright then back at Zander. "Are you sure?"

"Sure, I'm sure. What time is it anyway, Doc?"

"Ten-thirty," the doctor answered.

"Yeah, Ma, you gotta get up at six. Go home and get some sleep."

"Yeah, maybe I better." She rapidly grabbed her things, because the longer she stayed, the more difficult it would be to leave. "Come here, sweetie," she said as she stood up. When Zander walked over, she put her arms through the bars and held him as close as she could. "Happy birthday, sweetheart." She started to cry. "I'm sorry."

"It's okay, Ma," Zander soothed her.

She released him, picked up her purse, and practically ran down the hall.

"Well, Zander, I should go, too…" Dr. Bright said.

"Hey, Doc, could ja stay a few more minutes?" the boy asked.

"Sure." He sat down on the chair vacated by Sharon. "What's up?"

"Well… there's somethin' I wanted to tell ya."

Dr. Bright sensed it was something big because Zander was staring at the ground. Then, as if awoken from a trance, the boy began dredging up all the lies he had told in therapy. Like a kid at confession hoping to prolong his penance, he started with the smaller lies. First, Zander and Dawn hadn't bumped into each other on the street that time Dr. Bright had salmonella. Rather, she had called him "out of the blue." Then, Zander shifted gears and started talking about Dawn's cocaine addiction. But, Dr. Bright sensed there was something more to their chance encounter, because Zander never used hackneyed phrases like "out of the blue." Also, the boy had sped away from the topic a little too quickly.

When asked what had prompted Dawn's phone call, Zander's eyes rolled around like marbles, and he begrudgingly began to speak. It seems that Dawn had stolen Dr. Bright's appointment book, found Zander's number, and called him. Then, he sped off down the road of the topic of her addiction again, leaving Dr. Bright in a cloud of confusion.

"That's what I been trying to tell ya, Doc. She's a big coke whore."

"Yeah… but why my appointment book?" Dr. Bright asked.

"She figured some a' your clients might be drug addicts tryin' to quit usin' cause usually those are the dudes who keep a little stash."

"So she was looking for someone in recovery?" Dr. Bright said, still trying to figure it out. "And she'd buy their stash?"

"Or get 'em to do it with her. 'Cuz people who just quit don't have much willpower." Zander looked back down at the floor. "And maybe she thought she'd find some new daddy. Ya know? Someone to take care a' her. Buy her things."

"And in return…" Dr. Bright began.

"C'mon, Doc," he laughed. "Do I gotta draw ya a picture?"

Dr. Bright thought of those days when Dawn had dressed provocatively.

"An' I ain't lyin', either."

"No, I know you're not, Zander."

"The only reason I didn't tell ya before was…" the teen looked down at the floor.

"It's okay, Zander. You don't have to say."

"No, I wanna say… it's… I felt bad. I mean you'd been so good to us, and we screwed you over."

"But you didn't steal it," Dr. Bright consoled him.

"Yeah, but I knew about it." He looked up. "I mean, that's how she got my number."

"Well, it's not your fault. But do you know who else she might've called?"

"Not really. She did hook up with one guy, though. Some accountant I think."

Dr. Bright leaned back in his chair and thought about Stan flying over his desk.

"Do you know how long she had my book for?" Dr. Bright asked.

"Nah, not really. I know she xeroxed the pages before she snuck it back in."

"Jesus!" the doctor exclaimed. "Why didn't she just write down the numbers?" Not that this would've been any better.

"I dunno. She's fucked up like that. Likes to keep reminders, ya know? Used to show me all kinds a' crap. Credit cards she stole from guys. A silver cigarette case. Lots a' stuff."

Dr. Bright saw Officer Evans down the hall pointing to his watch. "Look, Zander," he said, looking at his own watch. "I think I better get going." He put the presents in his briefcase. "I'll see you tomorrow, okay?"

"Okay."

When Dr. Bright got back to his apartment, he looked at his appointment book. He thought of Stan punching him, and he realized it was really Dawn who had punched him. Because if Stan hadn't been strung out from the cocaine she'd gotten him back into, and if he hadn't been in a state of shock because his Barbie doll had killed a man, he probably wouldn't have resorted to violence. And when he thought of Stan, Zander, and Mickey, he started to realize that Dawn was like a poisonous flower destroying everything she touched.

☙

By now, the desk sergeant at The Tombs knew Dr. Bright and he called upstairs without being asked when the psychologist walked in the following morning. Detective Kelly was off-duty and Officer Serena Sanchez, the guard who had made an omelet with his head, was on her way down to escort him to Tampon Bay. In anticipation of her arrival, Dr. Bright's mind reflexively summoned disparaging images of the softball-playing prison guard—a beefy, masculine thing with a double chin and thick fingers; however, his assumptions shattered like glass when she rounded the corner. Serena was probably twenty-five years old with a face like Halle Berry's, only prettier, if that's possible. She had one of those bodies God had sculpted with an erection. Moments later, in the elevator, she apologized for hitting him, and Dr. Bright could tell her heart felt worse than his head ever had.

"Hey, listen, Officer…"

"Call me Serena," she politely interrupted.

"Serena," Dr. Bright continued. "You were just doing your job."

"I know, Doctor. I just hate violence. Understand?" She looked around the elevator like it was crowded with bad memories. "I just want it all to stop."

The elevator doors opened on the word "stop," as if granting Serena's request. Tampon Bay, a receptacle of violence, emerged in all its glory—dead hands on the bars, walls the color of sunburned skin, the smell of urine beneath bleach. Dawn was sitting on her cot reading when Dr. Bright approached. She seemed to be deeply absorbed in her magazine and she had a curious expression on her face—a mixture of contentment and intrigue, which seemed at odds with her grim surroundings. In fact, she seemed completely oblivious to the gloomy atmosphere until she saw Dr. Bright and her demeanor became a picture of pain and suffering.

After Officer Sanchez left, Dawn told Dr. Bright about her parents' sudden trip to Europe. She said they always went there when her mother was "about to break." When asked how she felt about their departure, Dawn said she was "used to abandonment." Without any segue, she asked Dr. Bright if he'd seen the "Invisible Boy," whom he correctly assumed was Zander, because his name hadn't been in the papers, while hers had been plastered all over. Strangely, Dawn seemed much more concerned with Zander's lack of exposure than she did about her alleged crime. She discussed the boy's culpability with the poise of a politician. Yet, when questioned about her own involvement, she turned as white as a ghost.

"I'm sorry, Dawn," said Dr. Bright. "Maybe it's too much to talk about right now."

"No, no," she said, closing her eyes. "It's just that I haven't really thought about it since that night."

The yellow balloon from Mr. Miller's eye appeared for one second in Dr. Bright's mind.

"It's hard," she said, with her eyes still closed, "when people keep telling you what you did."

"Yeah, I know." He tried to make his voice soft.

"Because, it's kind of like…" She rubbed her knees with her hands. "You forget what really happened, cause everyone keeps telling you what you did."

Her eyeballs searching behind their lids were like fingertips under silk.

"I remember drinking with the guy, and he grabbed me… no, wait. First, he asked me if I wanted to get high," she said, clutching her knees. "Then, I asked the guy if Zander could come along, but he said no… so I whispered for Zander to follow us, but he didn't…" She cringed like she was expecting an explosion.

"It's okay, Dawn," Dr. Bright comforted her.

"He…" Her eyeballs searching frantically. "… grabbed me… and I…" Her lower lip started to melt. "I… told him to stop, but he wouldn't." Tears dripped from her closed eyes. "So I…" She suddenly let out a scream, and within seconds Officer Sanchez was in the cell holding a sobbing Dawn like an infant in her arms.

"Come on, Dawn," she said, patting her back. "That's right… just breathe, baby… that's right." And while soothing the girl, the officer threw a dubious look at Dr. Bright meant to cast doubt on the authenticity of Dawn's tears.

ɔ

Later that day, as Dr. Bright was seeing Alex out the door after a session, Evelyn pulled up in her Saab. The doctor signaled that his next client had arrived and wished him a fond farewell. However, rather than getting the hint, Alex unwrapped another Tootsie Roll and scanned the street. Evelyn emerged from her car with a wave, and Alex, thinking the gesture was intended for him, shook his arm in the air. When she reached the curb the two clients exchanged amorous glances. After going inside, Dr. Bright looked out the window and saw Alex staring at the closed door.

For the first ten minutes, Evelyn bubbled over with questions about Alex—what was his name? Where did he live? What did he do? Was he married? Normally, Dr. Bright wouldn't relinquish private information about another client. However, an extraordinary thing was happening, so he altered his policy—Alex was the first man Evelyn had found interesting that wasn't spun from the loom of her imagination, and the doctor didn't want to close the door on her first step into reality. But, because he didn't want Evelyn's hopes dashed either, he slipped a few caveats into their conversation, to which she took great offense.

"I'm not six years old, Doctor," she said reproachfully.

"I know that, Evelyn," he replied. "I'm just looking out for you."

"You're also looking out for you." She let that statement stand alone for a moment. "But the problem is you think I'm as fragile as a China doll, and I'm not. See, when I first came here…" She glanced at the wall, as though the memory of herself was there. "… I was very fragile, and you," she said, looking back at Dr. Bright, "were so kind and sweet. You handled my feelings with velvet gloves… which is just what I needed, back then… but I don't need that anymore. No, wait a minute, damn it!" She looked down at the floor. "That's not what I wanted to say."

"Well… what did you want to say, Evelyn?" Dr. Bright asked.

"It's not that I don't need it anymore," she said, looking up. "I don't want it anymore!" The happiness of springtime poured into her eyes, "I said it! And you're not mad… or hurt, Doctor?"

"No, Evelyn," he replied. "I think it's wonderful."

"I'm so glad, and I…" she said, looking around the room as though flowers were everywhere. "I've got something else to tell you."

"Okay," he said.

"Well, it's just that for the last couple weeks, I've felt a little stifled here."

Dr. Bright motioned for her to keep talking.

"I feel like I've changed, but you've still been treating me the same way. Like that time we looked at my pictures, remember? Well, I know you thought I was resisting talking about my parents, my childhood, my weight, but the fact is, I've come to terms with all that stuff, and I was annoyed with you for making me dig up all those things I'd already laid to rest."

Dr. Bright stayed as silent as his chair.

"My father was a cruel bastard, and my mother was a drunk. Is talking about it more going to change it?" She looked out the window. "I think too many people dwell in the past, so they don't have to live in the present. At least I know that's what I've been doing for the past fourteen years. And all this bullshit about losing fifty pounds. I mean, it's all the same thing."

"How so, Evelyn?" Dr. Bright inquired.

"Because it's all avoidance. If I keep thinking about the fifty pounds I'm *going* to lose, then I'm living in the future, because I'm focusing on what I'm *going* to do instead of what I'm doing right now. And it's all a big pipe dream anyway, this magical day in the future where I'm skinny and beautiful, where I matter. See, I'm beautiful and important right now, but that's the hardest thing."

"What's the hardest thing, Evelyn?"

"To admit that I'm beautiful and important." A tear slipped down her cheek, but she instantly wiped it away. "And I'm not going to cry, either."

"Why not?" he asked.

"Because I'm happy, goddamn it!" She was crying and laughing at the same time. "Do you believe that I'm happy?"

"Yes, Evelyn," he replied. "I most certainly do."

14

Due to an influx of new clients, Dr. Bright hadn't seen Zander and Dawn as often. He had been visiting them at The Tombs during their appointed times, but now new patients had taken those spots and getting down to Lower Manhattan had become difficult. However, Detective Kelly called one morning and asked him to stop down. Apparently, Zander wanted to see him, and because one of his new clients was on vacation, the doctor was able to go.

Passing through the threatening door that led to Bates Motel, Dr. Bright heard the muffled sounds of music, and he soon realized that it was coming from Zander's cell. Ever since he had made friends with Officer Evans, Zander had the unprecedented privilege of having an iPod, while the rest of the guys were lucky to have magazines. Dr. Bright had to rap on the bars a few times to get his attention.

"Doc!" Zander sat up and tore the headphones off his head. "I fuckin' hate that!"

"Sorry, Zander," the doctor apologized.

The boy looked around the cell like it was all new to him.

"What were you listening to, Zander?"

"Huh? Oh… Pearl Jam," the boy responded.

Feeling the need to create a bridge between them, Dr. Bright said, "I like Pearl Jam."

Zander's frown twisted into a crooked smile. "Get the fuck outta here, Doc. What songs do you like?"

"I like 'Better Man,' 'Black,' 'Daughter,'" the doctor replied.

"'Daughter,'" Zander scoffed, dismissing the tune with a wave of his hand. "Radio hit."

"Radio hit?" Dr. Bright inquired.

"Yeah, they always have a hit on there for the little whores. Then, all the little whores tell their little whore friends, so they run out an' buy it, too."

"Whores?" Dr. Bright asked.

"Yeah, Doc. *Whores*," Zander emphasized the disparaging term. "Know what I mean? Bitches, cunts, clams, cows, wenches, pigs, sluts?"

"Oh, I see," the doctor curtly replied.

"What's a matter, Doc? Don't ya like my names for sex kittens?"

"No, Zander. Actually, I don't."

The boy stood up. "Is this what you're gonna do today, Doc? Talk about girls' rights an' crap like that? 'Cause if you are, you can just turn right the fuck around and go home 'cause I don't need to sit here and listen to that." His eyes were the color of the ocean floor at night. "It's easy for you. You get to leave here tonight, but I gotta stay! Do you hear me? I gotta fuckin' stay!"

"Okay, Zander, you're right, you're right," said Dr. Bright, realizing in a few sad seconds that several important things had happened to the boy. First, his stay here had poured more concrete around his heart. And second, perhaps more importantly, the boy's experience with Dawn had radically changed his views about women. In the past, Dr. Bright had heard countless invectives pour out of Zander's mouth about homosexuals, hermaphrodites, bisexuals, Latinos, Guatemalans, Greek waiters, and Middle Eastern cab drivers. However, he had never heard Zander chew up and spit out as many women as he had in recent weeks. The doctor still didn't take Zander's ethnocentric or homophobic comments seriously, because most of the time with teenagers these kinds of remarks weren't harbingers of life-long bigotry. They were more akin to fashion statements, like spiked hair or nose rings, which would eventually be discarded. But the tone of Zander's voice when he talked about women was venomous and hateful.

"Fuckin' people don't know how different shit is when you can't leave. Fuckin' lawyer's the same way. Keeps tellin' me to keep my chin up. What the fuck does that mean?"

"I don't know, Zander. I think maybe he wants you to try and stay positive."

"How the fuck am I supposed to do that? Look at this fuckin' place!"

"I know," the doctor agreed.

"No, ya don't know, Doc! Look! Look the fuck around!" the boy screamed.

Dr. Bright looked around. He saw a long gray line of cells. A floor the color of a polluted lake and a window at the end of the hall with the sad light of evening trapped behind the bars.

Exhausted, Zander lay down on his cot as hostile silence crept down the hall. Reflexively, the boy began talking about his lawyer's strategy, and how it would be better if they tried him as a juvenile. How it would be at least another six months before the thing went to trial. But his words didn't have a hint of sincerity, and Dr. Bright could tell there was something else Zander wanted to say.

"Hey, Doc, ya know this might sound stupid, but I'm looking forward to the trial."

"That doesn't sound stupid, Zander," Dr. Bright said. "I'm sure this in-between time stinks."

"Yeah, it does stink. But that ain't what I mean... I mean... I want to be punished. Ya know, all this stuff they say about your conscience? It's true. My lawyer keeps sayin' I got the right attitude... that if the judge sees I feel bad, he'll go easy on me. But I don't want him to go easy on me..." He stared at the floor.

"Is there more you wanted to say, Zander?"

"Yeah. I been kinda thinkin' about the trial, picturing it ya know? And, like, I picture the lawyers arguin' and the judge hittin' his desk with that wooden thing and the jury... and I see myself on the stand... and Dawn on the stand." He swallowed and wiped his forehead. "Yeah, well anyway," he said, his voice getting a little thinner. "I realized somethin' yesterday..."

"What did you realize?" Dr. Bright asked.

"This whole time I been picturing me on the stand and my mom on the stand and you on the stand and Dawn on the stand..." He was straining to keep his voice together. "I been picturing him there, too."

"Him?"

"The dude... Mickey," the boy swallowed. "And yesterday, when I was out in the yard for recreation, lookin' up at the clouds, it hit me..."

"What hit you?"

"We stole that dude's clouds."

A stifling silence descended for a moment, and then Zander continued.

"We stole his clouds, his sun, his Central Park… we stole everything from that dude. And he can't ever get it back." He rolled over and faced the wall.

As Zander lay there and the heavy minutes passed, Dr. Bright quietly explained to him that the pain he felt was good because he was acknowledging his feelings. Then, after another period of thick emptiness, the doctor asked him how he had felt while looking up at those clouds. At first, Zander didn't respond, and because he was facing the wall, Dr. Bright thought he might have fallen asleep. But, as that choking silence crept in again, Zander started talking. He said it was as if the clouds had been enormous hands pressing him into the ground. He said if it weren't for the bell summoning them to lunch, he would have "stayed in the yard forever." Zander said he was "ashamed" of the next thing he'd felt. When asked if that feeling had been relief, the boy nodded his head up and down.

Dr. Bright knew Zander was crucifying himself for what he'd done. Subconsciously, the boy needed the nails to be driven into his hands, the imaginary mob to throw stones, and the thorns to rip into his temples. When relief caressed his young heart, it was uncomfortable because he'd dipped into the thing he'd been dreading most—the truth. When Dr. Bright explained this to him, Zander rolled over with moist eyes of acceptance. As Dr. Bright knew the time was ripe for this discussion, he continued with the next piece, the verbal reality—he'd have to talk about the night of the murder. Upon hearing this, the boy put his head in his hands because to him this meant going back to that night of terror. That night now existed only in his horrifying memory.

"Listen to me, Zander. What happened that night is over now. Those images in your mind are just pictures, snapshots. They can't hurt you. It's just like watching a scary movie."

"Fuckin' *really* scary movie," the teen said in a muffled voice.

"Okay, but what do you see right now?" Dr. Bright asked.

"Whaddya mean, what do I see right now?" He looked up at Dr. Bright again.

"What… do… you… see?" The doctor spaced out his words.

Zander shot back, "I see you, ya fuckin' prick! Whaddya expect me to see?"

"Exactly!" the doctor responded. "You see me, not the scary movie. That means you're in control, not the pictures. You can shut them off whenever you want to."

The boy's eyes drifted up to the ceiling.

"You've got the remote control, Zander."

"Not when I'm dreamin' I don't."

"Well, you're right, because then your subconscious has the remote. See, Zander, when a person experiences something as frightening as that night, the mind desperately needs to process what happened. And in your case, your mind needs to watch that scary movie. But because you won't watch it during the day, your subconscious plays it at night."

The boy's face twisted in bewilderment, and the doctor continued to explain.

"See, consciously you can't accept those pictures. They're not like little sips of water you can just swallow. When you're awake, your mind rejects them because they're too scary."

One of Zander's eyes chaotically blinked, while the other was a wide-open door.

"Just like how your stomach digests food…" Dr. Bright deliberately cut off his sentence to see if Zander was still listening.

"Yeah, what about my stomach, Doc?"

"Well, just like how your stomach digests food, your mind digests events in your life. But some of these events are like pieces of bad chicken."

Zander scowled at him like *he* was a piece of bad chicken.

"And," Dr. Bright continued, "when your stomach rejects the foul meat…"

The boy interrupted, "You fuckin' puke and shit for three days. Fuckin' diarrhea starts to look like piss. Fuckin' dick and butt hole get confused. Shit starts coming out your dick."

"Exactly, and why?" the doctor probed.

"Cause jour stomach don't like dee bad cheeckin." He smirked and said in a low accented voice, "Stomach say 'get out, bad cheeckin.'"

"Yes, Zander, just like your mind says, 'get out' to traumatic events."

The fragile smile fell off the boy's face. "So, like, my mind has to puke and shit?"

"That's right," Dr. Bright acknowledged.

Zander had been treading cautiously into the wilderness of his emotions. But when asked to talk about Dawn, he became loquacious. He said that at first she'd called him to find out if he was still selling Ritalin, which, Dr. Bright found out, was one of the "hottest drugs" on the market. It seems that the "legal stuff" was not only stronger than the "illegal stuff," but it was easier to get and easier to deal. Zander said that he had deliberately fucked around in class and had failed tests to get labeled ADHD. Then, he'd been prescribed Ritalin. With pride in his sails, he explained how he had cleared five hundred bucks in his first month selling the prescription drug. Then, he took the money, bought cocaine and marijuana, and sold these as well.

One thing the teenage tandem shared in their cell block therapy sessions was a desire to deride the other one. Dawn complained about Zander's lack of exposure in the media, while Zander seemed obsessed with Dawn's promiscuity. The boy told Dr. Bright how she had been one of his best customers. Although he hadn't made much money off Dawn because she paid for most of her drugs with sex, she had been an asset to Zander's business because she attracted customers like "the accountant." Zander clearly remembered the first time he had sold cocaine to Stan because Dawn had furtively filmed the transaction with her iPhone. She planned on destroying the man's life "for the hell of it" by posting the video on social media, but she lost all interest in the financier when she met her "Sugar Daddy" back in December. According to Zander, when Mickey came around last Christmas, Dawn discarded him, L Train, and Stan as if they'd been old toys because Mickey had endless supplies of cash and coke which he lavished on his "princess."

During January and February, Dawn had "disappeared." She had sent Zander a few texts detailing her sexual escapades with Mickey, but aside from those she had "totally dipped." However, sometime in March, Dawn began coming around again. She said that she had grown tired of Mickey, but Zander knew that it was the other way around. For, one night while intoxicated, Dawn had confessed that the drug dealer had kicked her out of his apartment, but by the next morning she had forgotten her drunken omission and Zander was willing to go along with her fabricated version of events. Then, on Saint Patrick's Day, they saw Mickey at the parade with some "new bitch" on his arm and Dawn "went ballistic." She threw a green beer at the dope peddler, tackled the girl, and punched her in the face. It took Zander and L Train several minutes to pull their enraged friend off her supine victim, and in her fury, Dawn looked like "an animal"—her lips were dripping with spit and her eyes were pits of molten lava.

By the time they got to Strawberry Fields, she had "become Dawn again." With tears falling from her pretty blue eyes, she told the boys that Mickey had held her captive for two months. She said that he had beaten her, fucked her up the ass, and kept her locked in a closet when he went out. Zander and L Train exchanged several incredulous glances during her preposterous tale, but neither one openly challenged her claims. Suddenly, a blast of Irish music from a car on Central Park West prompted Dawn to get up and sing "Danny Boy" in the middle of the Imagine Circle as if the upsetting incident with Mickey hadn't happened.

"Did you see Mickey again that day?" Dr. Bright inquired.

"No… we didn't see him again until…" the boy paused, "*that* night."

Zander explained that a few weeks later, Dawn had asked him to meet her at Strawberry Fields with the promise of a "big surprise," and when she showed up wearing a tight black mini skirt and a lace tank top, his heart filled with joy because he thought she had dressed up for him. Yet, within five minutes his heart sank because Mickey showed up and planted a "big, wet kiss on her." Then, after playing "grab-ass" on the bench next to Zander for a while, the two walked off toward the Lake.

"So, what did you do then, Zander?" Dr. Bright asked.

"Me?" the boy responded. "I sat there for a while. Then, I started to leave. That's when I heard the screaming."

"Screaming?" the doctor inquired.

"Yeah, man. Scariest shit you ever heard in your life." Zander dropped his head into his hands.

"Why was Dawn screaming?" the doctor inquired.

"Dawn?!" The teen looked up. "She wasn't screamin' man! It was *him* screamin'!" He cringed like he was hearing it all again. "The poor motherfucker."

A cough from a distant cell reminded Dr. Bright that a world outside of Zander's nightmare still existed.

"Fuckin' sounded like a dog getting killed… dude was fuckin' howling." The boy grabbed his face with his hands.

"What did you do?" Dr. Bright asked.

"Well, at first, I just kinda sat there. But then, I heard her call my name, so I went lookin' for 'em. I couldn't find 'em."

"So the screaming had stopped?" Dr. Bright asked.

"Yeah, the screaming stopped." Zander's eyes drifted up to the ceiling. "And ya know something, Doc? That was the scariest time. Those few minutes when it was quiet and I couldn't find her."

Dr. Bright imagined a pitch-black Central Park. So black, all the figures and shapes were gone—the Bethesda Fountain, the Promenade, the Boat House, Cherry Hill— all erased by the unrelenting darkness.

"But then I heard… groanin'… felt like lightning hit me right in the gut, it scared me so much… sounded like a fuckin' huge bullfrog." Zander looked at Dr. Bright, "You know the way bullfrogs sound, Doc? How they almost sound like they're burping?"

"Yeah, yeah…" Dr. Bright urged him to continue.

"Well, that's what I heard… but the burps were like… filled with fluid… like the frog was lying on the shore with half his head in the water. Anyway, I sorta didn't know what else to do, so I kept searchin' for 'em and the bullfrog sound got louder… but then it would get quieter… like I'd be close, but then not… and my fuckin' sneaks were all full a' mud and I almost started thinking everything was okay… like maybe they got into a little fight, but then everything was cool… but then…" He paused and looked down at the floor.

"It's okay, Zander, take your time." Dr. Bright noticed beads of sweat on the boy's forehead.

"But then I saw her, man." He rubbed his clammy hands together. "She was kneeling next to the guy… blood all over her face and arms… ever seen that movie *Carrie,* Doc?" He looked up.

"Yes," Dr. Bright reluctantly recalled Sissy Spacek's performance in the grisly film.

"Well," the boy continued, "she looked like that Carrie chick… all fuckin' bloody and crazy."

Dr. Bright pictured Dawn drenched in blood next to a crimson corpse.

"At first, I didn't know what she was kneeling next to… thought it was a sleeping bag some faggot left behind, but then…" he said, using his t-shirt to wipe his face, "the fuckin' scariest thing happened…"

If the scariest thing wasn't liquid screams or Dawn covered in blood, thought Dr. Bright, then I'm in for a horrible surprise.

"The fuckin' dude got up," Zander said.

"What?" the doctor exclaimed incredulously.

The teen persisted, "I don't know how he done it, but the next thing I know he's all over her…"

The bloody corpse in Dr. Bright's mind stood up with yellow balloons coming out of its eyes and pink organs spilling out of its sides. "But he was cut to ribbons," he said aloud to quell the vision.

"Nah… not yet he wasn't," Zander continued. "She stabbed him pretty good a couple a times… but then I…" He wiped his face with his shirt again. "I finished him off… See, Doc, he had her by the throat… an' she was screaming… an' I saw the blade beside her, so I just started cuttin'. Fuckin' stabbed him five times in the back, and he still wasn't off her. So I picked up a rock and smashed him in the head… that made him drop. I was afraid he was gonna get up again, so I hit him a few more times. Fuckin' head cracked like a walnut man… some yellow shit came out of his ear and eye… and when he didn't have a face no more, I dropped the rock and just started stabbin' the motherfucker again… that's when Dawn said the thing everyone read about…"

"The thing?" Dr. Bright asked.

"Yeah… she said, 'Gut him, he'll sink,' or somethin' like that. An', like, I heard what she said, but her words didn't mean nothin' to me, cause I figured if I stabbed him enough, he'd go away… disappear, ya know? But he didn't… he just kept getting uglier an uglier… like when you step in dog shit and try to wipe it off, but it keeps coming off on your carpet… ya know what I mean, Doc?"

"Yes…" Dr. Bright agreed to keep Zander's confession flowing.

"Well, that was him, man," the teen continued. "Couldn't wipe him off. He just kept spreadin' all over everything. So we decided to roll him into the lake, but when we finally got him in there, the motherfucker floated, so we both swam out an' pulled him back out. That's when we made them really big holes… see man, cause to us it was like he was still fightin'… ya know, threatening to nark on us, so it was almost like fun fuckin' him up. Started laughin' one time 'cause Dawn said it was like cuttin' cookie dough… but then there was nothin' left to cut, man… dude was like a bowl a chili… so we rolled him back into the water, and this time he sank…"

The halo of fluorescent light around Zander's sixteen-year-old face made this horrifically violent and disturbing story seem all the more grotesque. And, as Dr. Bright looked at this murderer who didn't even have a driver's license yet, thoughts fell into his head—Zander was only sixteen. He wasn't even old enough to go to an R-rated movie by himself, or buy cigarettes. Yet, he'd committed the most horrible crime imaginable in the most savage way possible. But, Dr. Bright thought, sixteen-year-olds don't murder people. They cheat on tests and play video games; they don't stab people to death.

Zander picked up his story: He and Dawn had left the scene and were walking back to her apartment. Central Park's Great Lawn had been lit up by a moon as bright as the sun, and it was here that the reality of their crime finally hit the boy. It was in the luminous clearing that Zander had first seen the bright red blood all over his hands, which had previously looked black. But, the moon had thrown an even more revealing light on Dawn.

Zander said, "I mean, like, right then I realized I committed that crime by myself... like, there was no one else in it with me."

"But Dawn did it with you," Dr. Bright reminded him.

"Yeah, but no, she didn't." He opened his big black eyes. "She ain't a fuckin' human being, Doc... she ain't got no fuckin' heart. I was on my hands and knees pukin' my guts out, and she was standin' there laughin' at me... callin' me a big fuckin' pussy and a mama's boy with the blood of this fuckin' dead dude all over her. And then, I realized... it's like if you killed a dude with a pack of wolves, the wolves ain't responsible, cause they're just eatin'. And that's all she was doin', man... just eatin'..."

Dr. Bright offered, "Zander, could it be that Dawn was putting on an act? You know, pretending to be tough to hide how scared she was? Or could she have been in a state of shock?"

"Aw man." The boy was still looking down. "If you coulda seen her all covered in that dude's blood, laughin', pointin', yellin'… Nah man, that weren't no act… an' the whole way back to her building, pointin', laughin'… callin' me a little bitch… askin' people we saw in the street if they wanted to buy some blood. Fuckin' scariest hoe I ever seen in my life, Doc."

"Dawn asked people if they wanted to buy blood?" Doctor Bright asked.

"Oh yeah, man," Zander replied. "It was all a big joke to her."

"Zander, what kind of drugs were you guys on that night?" Dr. Bright inquired.

"Just beer and weed, man, and that's the thing! If we'd a' been on acid or somethin' I could see, but we weren't even trippin', Doc. That was all her!"

Then, perhaps sensing his psychologist's inability to grasp the full nature of Dawn's wickedness, Zander shared a detail that had been festering like an open wound inside him—with downcast eyes he said that Dawn had bragged about having sex with Dr. Bright in his office. The man felt nauseous as Zander recounted her fabricated details about all the times they had "fucked on his desk." What really took the cake was the story about the morning they "made it" in her bedroom when her father was "just outside the door."

Then, something occurred to Dr. Bright. Telling those lies wasn't simply a way for Dawn to foment trouble. Seeing Zander's suspicious eyes stuck to the floor made the doctor sense a much darker motive—Dawn saw herself drowning in an enormous dark ocean of pain and she wanted to pull as many people down with her as she could. She'd probably heard Zander mention Dr. Bright's name with admiration in his voice, and this had been more than she could bear. Zander's one strand of hope mirrored her own hopelessness. So she set out to destroy his therapy, the one positive thing in the boy's life.

"Look, Zander," Dr. Bright said, "I've got news for you. A minute ago, you called Dawn an animal."

"Yeah? So what?" The teen said defensively.

"Well, animals don't tell lies, and they don't try to destroy relationships."

Zander looked up at Dr. Bright.

"Dawn saw that you'd formed a bond with me, and she didn't like it. Because it meant you had something positive in your life, and it scared her."

"Scared her?" the boy asked.

"Yes. In you, she thought she had found someone to swirl down the toilet with. But the only people who swirl down the toilet are the people who've lost all hope, and you hadn't lost all hope yet."

"I see what ya mean. Like how they say, misery loves company."

"Misery *needs* company, Zander."

The boy squinted at Dr. Bright like he didn't understand.

"See, Zander, people on their way down crave companions. Otherwise, the fall to rock bottom is too frightening."

"Yeah, I know what ya mean. Probably why I hung around Dawn so much… can't say I ever really liked her… always knew she was a lyin' hoe. I don't know why, but I hung around her anyway… I guess shit gets too sad when you're by yourself."

The window at the end of the hall was covered as if by a dark hand. Now that Zander's yawns were sounding at thirty-second intervals, Dr. Bright decided it was time to go. Outside, the sky was dark but the clouds were still bright white. It was almost as if they had been dozing while the rest of the day had departed, and now they were wide awake in an unfamiliar sky. No one else seemed to notice this celestial aberration. For some reason, the doctor found great comfort in these lost, white clouds.

15

Zander's confession stirred up discord in Dr. Bright's heart, and he meditated on his turbulent feelings while waiting in Detective Kelly's office the following evening—he had known that Dawn was disturbed, but for some reason he was still having a hard time accepting the fact that there was murderer behind those pretty blue eyes. Part of his struggle, he realized, meant recognizing his own faulty judgment, but something else was preventing him from seeing the real Dawn.

"Okay, Doc, she's ready." Detective Kelly materialized in the doorway.

"All right." Dr. Bright started to get up, but the gumshoe motioned for him to stay seated.

"While you're here," the Detective began, "I've been meaning to ask ya something." He sat down at his desk. "I noticed that last spring ya started seeing Dawn twice a week."

"That's right," Dr. Bright replied.

"How come?" The cop's tone was more accusatory than the doctor was used to, and it rattled him a bit.

"Well, Lou..." he started to say then awkwardly corrected himself. "Mrs. Fontaine didn't think Dawn was making progress quickly enough, and decided twice a week would be better."

"Did ya think twice a week would help her?" the Detective asked.

"Well, sure... I mean, we'd been making some progress, but..."

"But Mrs. Fontaine didn't think so?"

"Well, that's not what I was going to say, but no, she didn't think so."

Kelly took a piece of paper off his desk and tried to scribble something down, but no ink appeared on the paper. "Okay, so..." he said, shaking the pen, "... at that time, you thought two sessions a week would help Dawn?"

"Here." Dr. Bright handed him one of his own pens, and for some odd reason, the exchange restored his confidence. "Yes, I did think it would help. I'd have to look at my records, but I think it was around that time when her appearance changed dramatically."

"How so, Doc?"

"Well, first of all, it looked like she hadn't been sleeping very well, because there were dark circles under her eyes. But she'd also lost some weight and her style went from Upper East Side to Upper East Side pretending to be Alphabet City."

Detective Kelly looked up from his paper and laughed. "From Upper East Side to Upper East Side pretending to be Alphabet City?"

"Yeah, you know," the doctor rejoined. "She'd dyed her hair and wore ripped jeans but carried a Prada handbag."

"I see." The detective started writing again. "And was it around that time when she first became associated with your client, Stan Palermo?" Kelly quickly looked up at Dr. Bright because he thought his question would catch him off guard.

"No idea," the doctor calmly replied. "I just found out about that myself."

"What?" Detective Kelly asked reproachfully. "When did ya find out Dawn hooked up with Stan Palermo?"

"Just a couple of nights ago. Why?"

"Because, Doc, that kinda information could be crucial to the case."

Dr. Bright said, "Well, since my records haven't been subpoenaed, I didn't think I was under any legal obligation to share every detail."

"Yeah, I know. But it's not like there's any doubt about who committed the murder anymore, so anything ya could tell us now would only be helpful to us." Detective Kelly looked at the floor. "And I think ya might as well know that Mrs. Fontaine is planning to file a suit against you. She claims that you and Dawn were having sexual relations."

"I see," said the doctor, now amused by the ludicrous accusation. "And when is she suggesting this illicit romance began?"

"I dunno, but, look," the Detective said, fidgeting with the pen in his hand, "there's something else I gotta ask ya…"

Dr. Bright interrupted him. "When did Howard and Louisa get back from France?"

"They're not back," Kelly replied. "Louisa finally returned my phone calls. Blabbed at me for two hours long distance."

"Jesus," the doctor sighed.

"So, Doc… I wanted to ask ya about Stan Palermo."

"What's he saying, that I had an affair with him, too?"

"No." Detective Kelly laughed. "But did you two have some kinda fight? He says ya hit him."

"*I* hit *him*! He hit me!" Dr. Bright shouted. "And I reported that right away!"

"Yeah, yeah, I know ya did," the Detective patted the air with his hands, "but can ya tell me what the fight was about?"

"We…" Dr. Bright remembered his ethical responsibilities regarding confidentiality. "No, I can't."

"Well, he won't tell us either and that's a problem, Doc. See, it looks like you two were fightin' over Dawn, and it kinda makes Dawn's allegations against you look more legit."

"I don't care what it looks like," Dr. Bright said defensively. "Her claims are completely fallacious."

"You're gonna care when the Fontaines' hotshot lawyer sinks his claws into you. And look, Doc, there's just one more thing… and it's only a piece of advice." Kelly rubbed his hands together like he was warming them over a fire. "I wouldn't visit Dawn anymore. I mean, they're already tryin' ta pile up evidence against ya. No need to help 'em shovel."

Dr. Bright considered the cop's suggestion and realized he was right, but he also felt compelled to see his client again. "Yeah, I see what you mean, Detective. But I think I'd like to see her just one more time, for some kind of professional closure."

Kelly handed back the borrowed pen and slowly stood up. He seemed tired as he grabbed the ring of keys off his desk and beckoned the doctor to follow him down a gloomy hall illuminated by the sickly glow of fluorescent lights, and after a few moments, they arrived at the door that led to Dawn's cellblock.

"Hey, Doc." Detective Kelly sluggishly sifted through his keys. "Are ya sure ya want ta do this? You seem kinda nervous."

"Yeah, I think it's important to make it clear to Dawn that I'm no longer her therapist."

"Ya sure? Cause the thing is, seems like she could probably figure that out, considerin' all the shit she's been sayin' about you and everybody else. And I mean, with the way she's acted here, you'll have plenty of people who don't believe a word she says who'll back you up. And Doc, did I tell ya the Fontaines are also suing Maxine and some a' the other guards…"

Dr. Bright remembered when Maxine had subdued Dawn. "Look, Detective, I was there for that… the kid had a bandage on her head the size of a bass drum. There was no need for Maxine to…"

"No, no, Doc. They're suin' her for sexual harassment. Dawn said Maxine and some a' the other guards beat her up because she wouldn't give in ta their sexual demands."

"Yes, well, I tried telling you before about Dawn's allegations, but you just called her a psychopath and dismissed it… I mean there might be some truth to…"

"Oh, my God!" Detective Kelly covered his mouth with a hand.

"What is it, Detective?" The doctor thought that perhaps Detective Kelly had just remembered something, like an appointment he was late for, or a newly uncovered piece of evidence.

"I really thought," he said, his voice muffled by his hand, "that you were just playin' with me, Doc. But ya really don't know, do ya? I mean, that crazy little bitch really has ya fooled."

"Detective, if you mean I haven't accepted the fact that she killed Mickey Miller… I have."

"No, ya haven't, Doc. We gotta get ya in to see her." He opened the door and practically pushed the doctor through. "Maybe there's still hope for ya."

The door closed and Dr. Bright was back in Tampon Bay. Once again painting her toenails, Dawn looked like a normal teenage girl in her bedroom at home.

"How long have you been standing there, Doctor?" she asked in a humid voice.

"I don't know, a few seconds maybe," he replied impassively.

"How do you like them?" She played an invisible piano with her toes.

"Very nice, Dawn."

"Which do you like better? These?" She raised her right foot. "Or these?" She raised her left foot.

"Is there a difference?" he asked.

"Yes, silly!" She put on that ingenuous little girl smile. "These," she said, raising her right foot again, "are succulent cherry, and these," she said, raising her left, "are luscious raspberry."

Looking into her baby blue eyes and noticing her slightly turned up nose that had not yet been chiseled by womanhood, Dr. Bright still couldn't picture her stabbing a man multiple times and rolling his lifeless body into Central Park Lake.

"Have you seen Zander recently, Doctor?" Dawn asked.

"Yes. I saw him last night," he replied.

She pushed out her bottom lip. "Why didn't you come see me first?"

"You were with your lawyer. And speaking of lawyers, Dawn, it looks like I'm going to need one real soon."

Suspicion visited her eyes for a moment then quickly disappeared. "Oh really?"

"Sure. You knew that, didn't you, Dawn?"

"How would I know that?" She batted her eyelashes.

"Well, you're the reason," the doctor said flatly.

Her eyes hit the floor with a thud.

"Why, Dawn?"

She didn't look up. "Why what?"

"Why would you say that you and I were having intimate relations?"

After a moment she said, "Well, it's true isn't it?"

"True? What's true?" the doctor asked.

"That you and I were having sex." She finally rested her eyes on him.

"Dawn that is an absolute lie."

"What do you mean?" She stretched her arms back so that her entire stomach was revealed.

"You know that is completely untrue," the doctor stated with a clear, firm tone.

She laughed mechanically.

"What's so funny, Dawn?" Dr. Bright asked.

"You are," she giggled. "Trying to be such a good boy… go ahead, it's okay if you want to look." She ran a finger across her stomach. "Or maybe my bad boy wants to see more." She started to raise her shirt with the tip of her finger.

"No, Dawn, I don't want to see anything," he said, then sighed with exhaustion.

"Are you sure?" she asked with sickening sweetness. "I mean, it's a little awkward with those bars, but I'm sure we could figure something out."

"No, Dawn," he said, closing his eyes.

"Aw. Wanna tell your baby what's wrong?"

"I'm sorry I couldn't help you," he said gravely.

"Sorry you couldn't help me?" She blinked a few times like a baby seeing something for the first time.

"I tried but… I didn't realize…" He stopped himself.

"Realize *what*?" When she said the word "what" it sounded like a bottle breaking.

Dr. Bright replied, "I didn't realize that you were in such bad shape."

"Bad shape?" Her voice suddenly sharpened. "Who's in bad shape?"

"You are, Dawn. Your condition is much more severe than I ever imagined."

"Well, what's my *condition*," her mouth lashed, "*Doctor*?"

"Well, I'd say you have sociopathic tendencies."

"You think I'm a *sociopath*?" Storm clouds gathered in her eyes.

"Yes. The thing is, in the beginning, I thought you were just love-starved and angry like so many kids today, but I was wrong. I misdiagnosed you because I let my feelings get in the way."

"Feelings?" She pounced on the word. "What feelings?"

"I felt sorry for you, Dawn. You and Zander. And I guess my feelings started to become a little more paternal than clinical."

"Paternal?" Her face twisted. "You mean you felt like my father?"

"No, I didn't feel like *your* father," he said, frustrated with the limits of his own verbal skills and her inability to identify with empathy. "I saw how badly life had treated you—your biological mother abandoned you, and in a way your adoptive mother did, too. And I should have paid more attention to all the warning signs. I failed you."

Dawn looked at him for a moment with what seemed to be sympathy, until she suddenly burst out laughing. "And I'm the sociopath?"

"I'm sorry, Dawn," he said, starting to walk away.

"Wait a second, wait a second. You still haven't taken it back."

"Taken what back?" Dr. Bright asked.

"You said I was a sociopath."

"Dawn, you asked what I thought was wrong with you, and that's my answer."

"Well, what makes me a sociopath, *Doctor*?" Her voice took on a weird metallic tambour.

"Because even after murdering a man, you're still playing your disgusting little games," the doctor replied with conviction.

She stood up and carefully walked towards the bars.

"Dawn," he continued, "Mickey Miller's murder doesn't bother you in the least. The only remorse you have stems from getting caught, and that total lack of empathy makes you a sociopath."

"Oh yeah?" She took another step towards him. "Well, you want to know what I think? I think you're a frustrated and fucked up old man, and you only listen to your clients' problems so you don't have to think about your own."

"Well, I'm sure you're right," he placated her.

"And the only reason you paid so much attention to me is because you wanted to fuck me!"

"You are *definitely* wrong about that, Dawn."

"Oh no, I'm not. Loved me like a daughter, huh? Want me to call you daddy?" Her batting lashes were grotesque against her malicious eyes. "Or maybe you want me to whimper while I'm sucking your cock?"

"Well, that does it for us, Dawn. Again, I'm sorry I couldn't help you."

"'Does it for us'? What do you mean 'does it for us'?" she asked.

"Dawn, I won't be your therapist anymore."

"How come?" She tried to make her face innocent again, but the venom wouldn't drain from her eyes.

"Dawn, there are certain boundaries that need to be respected in order for a therapeutic relationship like ours to function, and today, you've trampled over every one."

"How?" Her lower lip protruded again.

"How? The sexual solicitations, asking me if I want you to whimper while…"

The breeze of a smile that passed across her lips made him realize he was playing right into her hands.

"Not to mention the fact that your mother is suing me."

"Well," she said, running her finger down one of the bars in front of him, "that doesn't have to happen."

"It doesn't?" he asked.

"No." She grabbed the bar at the level of his crotch. "It's up to you. Start being nice to me again and I won't sue you."

"Start being nice? Dawn, what are you talking about?"

"Well, for one thing, I want you to stay my therapist, and for another thing…" she said, rubbing her clenched hand up and down the bar, "… I want you to stop lying."

"Lying?" he asked. "Lying about what?"

"Yes. I want you to take back what you said about me being a sociopath, and I want you to admit that you want to fuck me." Her wide-open eyes darkened like the windows of an abandoned house. For the first time, Dr. Bright saw the vast emptiness inside of her. Emptiness she'd been trying to fill throughout her life with sex, alcohol, drugs, and lies, until finally, when she could no longer bear the hunger, murder. But not even murder, the complete destruction of another human being, could satisfy her starving heart.

"Listen, Dawn, you've got a lot of work ahead of you, but it's going to be okay."

"You mean *we've* got a lot of work ahead of *us*." She corrected him.

"No, Dawn. I'm saying goodbye to you now."

"No!" She grabbed the bars with both hands. "You won't be saying goodbye!"

"Listen, kid." He took a step back. "I'm leaving."

"You might be leaving, but you're not saying goodbye!" She pressed her face between the bars. "Because your little boy's gonna take the rap for all of this and I'll be out of here in no time!"

He turned and walked away.

"Go on, daddy! Go on! 'Cuz pretty soon, your little girl is coming home!"

When Dr. Bright got home, he felt the hollow pain of disillusionment because he had misjudged Dawn, and now he knew it. Her pathology had been staring him in the face, but pride and an inflated sense of his own abilities had prevented him from seeing it. He had thought that emotional neglect had cast a darkness around her heart, and that helping her find the light of her own goodness was what she needed to heal, but he was wrong—tonight had shown him the severity of her illness, and he realized that he had lost her.

16

One morning in October, Dr. Bright saw a message blinking on his answering machine. After playing it, he heard a voice whose loveliness made his heart leap— "Doctor, it's Sharon Lee, Zander's mom. I'm sorry it's been so long since you've heard from me. Trying to work and deal with this trial has pretty much consumed me. Believe it or not, I'm also involved in another lawsuit trying to get Zander's father to help pay some of the bills. As usual, he's been trying to avoid paying a cent." Here, there was a silence during where it seemed she was trying to gain momentum for something. "The real reason I'm calling you is to tell you that you've been more than wonderful… wonderful doesn't even come close to what you've been… and I'm not good with words, but… if there are such things as angels, that's what you've been… and I can't even begin to tell you what it's meant to Zander." Here the allotted time for a message ran out, but she called right back. "Sorry about that, and I won't take up any more of your time, but I was wondering if you could visit Zander… he's not doing so well. He's anxious, depressed, and he won't say anything to me, but I know he's terrified about the trial… his friend there, Officer Evans, told me that he hasn't been eating or sleeping. He said that every time he walks by his cell, Zander's just sitting there on the edge of his cot with his head in his hands…" After a five-second pause she returned. "I know you're a busy man, and I wouldn't blame you if you never wanted to set foot in that place again, but he's suffering…"

Here the tape ran out again, so the rest of her sentence was lost but the sound of her voice illuminated Dr. Bright's heart like sunlight on a flower. It had been months since their passionate embrace, but her words rekindled his feelings, and he felt radiant inside. However, a cold shadow fell across his mood when he realized that their chance of a romance had died because they'd always remind one another of a night that both would want to forget.

It was dusk when Dr. Bright got to The Tombs. He hadn't seen Zander in a while, and something told him that this would be the last time. Detective Kelly wasn't there. Officer Sanchez wasn't either, and the unfamiliar guards made him feel uneasy. He felt out of place, like a ghost. Yet, seeing Zander slumped over on the edge of his cot in the same position Sharon had described made all of the doctor's uneasiness dissolve in a pool of pity. When Zander looked up, Dr. Bright saw why Sharon had been crying. The boy had lost weight, his skin was the color of skim milk, and he had a bandage on his forehead.

Before Dr. Bright could question him about his appearance, Zander looked up at him with pleading eyes and said that "thoughts keep busting into my head."

Especially at night, he said, the thoughts were "way too fuckin' pushy." He even told Dr. Bright his strategies for repelling the "fuckin' brain intruders." These methods included yelling at the intrusive thoughts, and when verbal intimidation didn't work, he'd smack his head on the wall, which accounted for the gauze bandage. Next, Zander asked Dr. Bright if he could get on a "lobotomy list." When the doctor asked why he'd want this procedure, the boy said he wanted to "get rid of his memories."

"That bitch played me. Know what I'm sayin'?" Zander pressed his fists into his eyes.

"I think so," Dr. Bright said softly.

"The only reason I started dealin' coke is so the fuckin' bitch'd hang out with me."

Dr. Bright's heart smote him; he realized that this grotesquely violent act had started as a case of unrequited teenage love.

Zander continued, "She made it seem like she liked me at first. Even hung outside your office and waited for me… called me all the time. I was fuckin' stupid." He lowered his head.

"Why is that stupid, Zander?" Dr. Bright asked.

"'Cause she was just playin' me the whole time and I couldn't see it, Doc. Even L Train, that fuckin' knucklehead, told me she was a player. But I thought he was just jealous." Two colorless tears ran down the boy's face. "Anyway, I lied to you, Doc."

"What did you lie about, Zander?"

"The whole thing. The stuff I told ya. You know, about that night… the night we…" He wiped the tears off his face. "It just don't seem real to me, Doc. I mean, I know it was me who did it, cause here I am… in jail… but it still don't seem like it was me. I mean, I almost feel like they got the wrong guy." He looked up at Dr. Bright with glassy eyes. "J'ever feel like that, Doc? Like you know you did somethin' but you don't feel like you did it?"

"Well, it sounds like you haven't fully accepted it yet, Zander, which is totally understandable. But in order for you to recover, you have to come to terms with what you did."

"How? I sit here every fuckin' night thinking about the shit."

"Yes, but you just said that you lied to me. And if you lied to me, you probably lied to yourself, too."

Zander's face darkened. "'Member how I told ya she collected stuff? You know, like your book with people's names an' stuff in it?"

"Yes," Dr. Bright affirmed.

"She collected suckers, too. Like a spider with flies, ya know? Me, the accountant, Mickey... we were all in Dawn's web. Even went after L Train, the poor fucker. But he wouldn't have nothin' to do with her... and that night, he tried to get me to leave with him, but I wouldn't.... Fuck!" He suddenly stood up. "I'd give anything if I could just go back there and listen to him!"

Instinct told Dr. Bright that without a little prompting, Zander's curtain would close. "So, L Train was there that night?"

"Yeah, he was there," he said, staring vacantly into a corner. "Member how I told ya I heard her screamin' and went lookin' for 'em?"

"Yes," the doctor answered.

"Well, that ain't what happened." The boy closed his eyes. "See, she an' that dude were kinda playin' touchy-feely all night, an' when I came back from takin' a piss one time, they were gone. See, an' I was getting all pissed off... sayin' I was gonna fuck him up, an' L Train was like, 'Dude, let's go, she's a hoe,' but I didn't wanna listen. But then, L Train was remindin' me of all the other shit she'd done to me, an' I realized he was right. But right when we were about to book, we heard 'em splashin' around in the water an' laughin'… they were fuckin' skinny dippin'… an' it was a full moon, so I could see 'em perfectly. He was feelin' her bare ass an' tits an' she was playin' Miss Keep Away, like she always does. Then, I think they heard someone comin', 'cuz they ran outta the water and started puttin' their clothes on, an' L Train's like, 'Dude, I'm outta here,' so he takes off.

"So I, like, sat there watchin' 'em 'til I couldn't take it no more. I bust outta the bushes, callin' him an asshole an' her a cunt right to their faces. But Dawn starts actin' all sweet an' shit, an' she's like, 'Zander, you've got it all wrong, we were just takin' a swim.' An' the dude's like, 'Yeah, calm down, Slugger. We're just friends.' An' there was somethin' about him lying like that to my face that really pissed me off, so I kicked him in the balls, an' when he bends over I go to kick him in the face, but he grabs my leg an' pulls me to the ground. An' he was a strong motherfucker, cause he, like, pins me in two seconds, says somethin' like 'That's enough now.' Then, outta nowhere, Dawn kicks him in the face… an' when he grabs his busted nose, she kicks him again. So, he falls off a' me, but he's got me in some kinda leg lock, an' won't let go… Dawn keeps kickin' him in the face every two seconds, but the fuckin' guy's holdin' me tighter and tighter.

"Then, Dawn pulls out her knife an' gives it to me an' I say to him, 'If you don't let me fuckin' go, I'm gonna fuckin' stab ya.' Dawn's like, 'Do it! Do it!' And I let him have one right in the hamstring, an' the dude fuckin' howls… but when I try to break free, he spins around like a crab an' grabs me around the knees… I'm like, 'Dude, let me go!' But he won't, so I let him have another, an'

Dawn's yellin', 'Finish him! Finish him!' So I plow one into his arm… he lets out this high-pitched scream, an' rolls off a' me… so I get up an' start runnin', but Dawn grabs me an' says, 'We can't leave him like this.'

"At first, I think she means we gotta help him, so I start walkin' back, but then she says, 'Yeah, we don't want him to snitch,' an' Doc, you shoulda seen her face." Zander looked off into the horrifying memory of it and scowled with clenched fists. "I mean, the moon was so bright it was like the sun up there, an' she had this look on her face. She was so fuckin' excited… then, I heard this groan… saw the dude tryin' to crawl away… but his hurt leg's draggin' behind him, an' his one arm gives out, so he collapses face-down on the ground. Then, a few seconds later, he gets himself back up an' starts crawlin' again. An' then…" Zander looked up at the fluorescent light in his cell. "Dawn starts throwin' big fuckin' rocks at the guy. One nails him hard in the head, an' he drops, an' Dawn says, 'I'm not lettin' that rat snitch on me, so either finish him off or gimme the fuckin' knife!' She looked so fuckin' crazy, Doc. Her eyes are all big an' bright an' her hair's all stuck to her face, so I give her the knife… she walks over there like she's goin' to buy a soda or something, an' stands over the guy for a few seconds. Then, she grabs the knife with both hands an' falls on the guy, an' he lets out this scream, so I take off. An' I'm running through the Rambles, an' I keep hearin' the fuckin' guy screamin'. When I get to Belvedere Castle, I decide to go back, an' then… I think I told ya the rest…"

"Well, yes, Zander, you did. But I think it might be good if you told me again," Dr. Bright said.

"Well…" He stood up in his cell and started pacing. "'Member I told ya how it got really quiet an' I couldn't find 'em… but then, I heard that half-dead bullfrog an'

found her kneelin' beside the guy covered in blood…
'member, Doc? Like that Carrie chick?"

"Yes, Zander, I remember."

"And then… aw man." Zander stopped and looked at the wall.

"And then he got up and attacked her, right?" Dr. Bright said, remembering the part that had been keeping him awake at night.

"Nah, man." The boy closed his eyes. "He didn't attack her. That was all bullshit. Fuckin' dude couldn't attack no one."

"So," the doctor rejoined, "was he dead then?"

"Well, we thought he was dead, so we started draggin' him towards the water, but he was too heavy, so we started rollin' him… an' then…" The boy grabbed his face with both hands.

"What is it, Zander?"

"All this junk starts spillin' out of him… out of his fuckin' eyes, his throat. An' I almost puked, but then we started pushin' harder, an' he rolled a little quicker 'til we finally got him into the water and shoved him away. An' man it was fuckin' creepy… the water was real still except where he was floatin'… but the moon was so bright, you could see him clear as day. We both swam out there an' pulled him back… that's when I kinda snapped…"

"What do you mean, Zander?"

"Well, man, I was real scared, but it was weird cause I was so fuckin' angry, too, 'cuz he didn't sink. That's when we made them big holes in his chest… Dawn was sayin' maybe we better cut off his face an' hands so nobody'd recognize him. So I slashed his face but Dawn was like, 'No, do it like this,' an' she cut off part of his nose and lips. Then, she tried to cut off one of his hands, but she couldn't do it, so she gave me the knife. An' I hacked at the bone till it broke, but it was takin' too much time, so we just rolled him back into the lake an' took off."

Zander and Dr. Bright were both startled by the sound of a closing door and the squeaking shoes of a guard coming down the hall.

"So then," Dr. Bright whispered, "you two went back to her apartment building, right?"

Zander held up a finger indicating a brief hiatus until the guard passed. Then his phantom universe reopened. "Yeah, but there was that thing on the Great Lawn… 'member, Doc?"

"Oh yes," the doctor replied, "you saw the blood on your hands and threw up."

"On my hands, shirt, knees, arms…" He cringed and closed his eyes like he was expecting to hear a loud crash.

"And Dawn laughed at you, right Zander? Is that what you're thinking about right now?"

"Yeah man," he said, a few tears dripping from his closed eyes, "that's what I'm thinkin' about… her standin' there in the fuckin' moonlight, pointin' at me, callin' me a pussy… an' it really hurt my feelings, ya know?"

"Yeah, I know," Dr. Bright said softly.

"An' I mean," he said, opening his big wet eyes, "she used ta tell me she loved me… an', like, I really believed her… that's why I went runnin' back there, ya know? I feel so fuckin' stupid… it was like the only thing that was keepin' me doin' all that bad shit. I knew it was wrong, but I thought she…"

And here, Zander broke down and cried. But because society tells men and boys it's not okay to cry, he rolled over and faced the wall. For a good half-hour or so, Dr. Bright watched the boy's shoulders shaking as every repressed tear passed through the portals of his eyes. As Zander braved the flood, dark clouds gathered in Dr. Bright, too.

It was becoming more and more clear that this grand scale tragedy was also the very small story of a boy's first broken heart. There was something about the simplicity of that, amidst this epidemic of chaos and violence, which was absolutely heartbreaking. After a while, Zander's body became as still as a corpse, and Dr. Bright realized that he was sleeping.

On the cab ride home, Dr. Bright remembered his first broken heart, and the walls of the present crumbled as he fell helplessly into the past—driving from Albany to Ocean City, New Jersey for their summer holiday, his father had always taken some convoluted route so that they could get the best view of the Manhattan skyline. He remembered driving forever down gray highways strewn with car dealerships, and his father pointing out landmarks like the Hudson River and Sleepy Hollow, but on this trip, Duncan had been focused on the yellow scarf wrapped around his mother's head. She'd fixed it so it covered her bald skull, and in the back two long pieces of silk blew in the wind. These scarves had become permanent fixtures of their home, but nobody talked about them. They had just appeared one day, and there was a color scheme to the scarves more startling than the scarves themselves. When she had first come home from the hospital, they'd been multicolored, neon numbers. But as time went by, they had gradually become more and more mellow.

Later her scarves had been green—pine, and later, a pale green that was almost blue. Then, they had run the gamut of red, from contemptuous rose to exhausted sunset. Her scarves were like the changing leaves on an October tree. It was as if subconsciously she had been preparing the family for her death, and they were now at the color he dreaded most—yellow.

But Duncan wasn't willing to let go of his mother without a fight, and although her hair had fallen out and her skin was the color of ashes, he was determined that she would get better. When he read that vegetables fought cancer cells, he made her salads and smoothies every day. Yet, this long drive had given him time to think, and he realized that he had to let his mother go. And right at that moment, when he had consciously begun preparing for her departure, Manhattan filled the front windshield and his father had yelled, "There she is!" Maybe it was partly due to his father's clumsy use of personification, but at that moment Duncan decided that Manhattan would be his new mother. One day, he'd wrap her skyscrapers and bridges around himself and be warm.

A long, slow curve had almost made it seem like Manhattan was turning until the island was finally behind them, and Duncan stared out the back windshield at his new home. For a long time, the city didn't get any smaller, and he remembered being filled with the fatuous hope that maybe, just maybe, they'd be able to see it from their hotel room in New Jersey. But the distance had begun to eat the city like the cancer that was eating his mother, and finally, the tall buildings merged with the thin ocean clouds.

17

In November, the city was once again plastered with images of Zander and Dawn. Just like when the story had broken last May, everywhere Dr. Bright turned, their faces stared back at him. He saw them on TV and in the newspapers. Some nights, while walking home, he'd see their crumbled-up faces in garbage cans, which clearly illustrated what most people felt should happen to them. And following a cryptic chain of events that he'd mentally pasted together from the media onslaught of updates on the murder case, Dr. Bright had learned that Dawn had been sentenced to serve ten years for manslaughter after accepting a dubious plea bargain in which she'd admitted to "assisting" Zander in the murder.

Without the blink of an eye, the wheels of injustice had turned. Because her high-priced lawyer had managed to manipulate the system, Dawn was on her way to a prison Upstate. With parole on the horizon for her, the murder trial, complete with media storm and public outcry, fell with a thud onto Zander's shoulders. Dr. Bright was sickened by this blatant miscarriage of justice—a vast pile of evidence had linked both to the scene of the crime, yet all Dawn had to do was point her finger at Zander, and now he was seen as the murderer. That was all it had taken. Dr. Bright even remembered reading in the paper that she had admitted to "ordering" Zander to "gut the body so it would sink." She'd also admitted to "helping him throw the body into the lake." Yet, somehow, the authorities had come to believe that this girl, with a well-documented history of violence, including at least one prior incident with a knife, had just stood by and watched as Zander wielded the weapon.

Dr. Bright certainly wasn't basing his opinions of the murder on Zander's story. Not only had the boy's two accounts been strikingly different, each was obviously full of glaring inaccuracies. Rather, Dr. Bright was basing his perceptions of the murder case on the enormous amount of evidence linking both teens to the crime, and on what he had learned from his therapeutic work with each of them. He knew that Dawn was an excellent actress who had fooled many people with her innocent routine. She had done so with himself, her family, Mickey, Stan, Zander, and now, apparently, the courts of New York. Yet, during the last session he'd had with her, she'd been kind enough to remove her mask. Dr. Bright had finally seen that he was dealing with a clear case of antisocial personality disorder, someone with a complete lack of empathy, and a blatant disregard for the rights and feelings of others.

On the first day of Zander's trial, one headline read "Baby-Face Butcher Goes on Trial for Central Park Slaying." Dr. Bright had never been more appalled by a simple grammatical shift. Since that fateful night in May, newspapers had always printed "Baby-Face Butchers." And, while the doctor hardly approved of the journalists' endeavors to make some sort of vulgar joke out of this tragedy, he at least appreciated the fact that they'd managed to get the number correct— "Butchers," indicating two. Now, however, it seemed like the New York media, usually cynical and suspicious, had eagerly swallowed Dawn's story, like naive children gobbling up tales of tooth fairies and flying reindeer. The article not only focused on Zander as the sole killer, but also reinforced its one-sided tirade by quoting, of all people, Dawn: "He just flipped out.... He just kept stabbing him.... He sliced his throat." Yes, magically, somehow almost overnight, Dawn had gone from prime suspect to leading witness. However, she hadn't totally left Zander hanging out to dry, for she'd supplied him with a motive: "I think he thought he saw Mr. Miller's arm around me and flew into a jealous rage." Aside from wondering which nice lawyer lent her the phrase "jealous rage," Dr. Bright very much admired the wording of "I think he thought." For it not only made Zander look like an impulsive psychotic, it also moved Dawn's pawn a few more spaces away from any wrongdoing that night, including any trace of sexual promiscuity. This got him thinking about the price of American justice—a court-appointed lawyer would probably lose the case. A moderately priced lawyer might get an acquittal. However, expensive attorneys will not only pull their clients out of the mud, they'll also hose them off and get the media to sprinkle rose dust, so that they're cleaner and more redolent than ever before. Translation: If you're poor, you'd better follow the narrow path of the law. And if you're rich—rich enough to afford high-priced lawyers to clean up your messes—you can do whatever you want.

On day two of the trial, Zander's lawyers were out to burn Dawn. The title "Girl Was out to Kill Someone" flew like a vulture above an article that cited the testimony of a surprise witness who'd been with Dawn hours before the murder. Holland Santos reported that he and Dawn had been "messing around" in Carl Schurz Park when she said, "I'm gonna kill someone before this night is over." Holland told reporters that he had thought it was a joke until she'd brandished a knife. The article continued to explain that a little later that evening, after buying beer at a convenience store, Dawn had turned to her companion with a "scary look" and said, "Come on, let's go. Let's kill somebody." This was when Santos "knew it was time to go home."

The evening newspaper editions revealed one more surprise witness who'd had the misfortune of crossing paths with Dawn that night. Lincoln Clark, an employee of Citibank, had stopped in that same convenience store on his way home from work and had seen Dawn buying beer. When interviewed, he told reporters that "out of nowhere, this girl just started screaming at me," and said that when he'd tried to ignore her, "she threw a bottle of spaghetti sauce past my head." To avoid further confrontation with the "obviously disturbed girl," Clark said he'd left the store. "I could tell she was crazy, so I left."

After reading the article, a few questions popped into Dr. Bright's mind. First of all, where were all of these witnesses when Dawn's plea bargain had been reached? Part of the hazy reasoning behind her dubious deal was that officials had "lacked evidence linking her to the crime," as well as a motive. But now, all of a sudden, there were two people who'd encountered her that night. One had heard her say she was going to kill somebody while she brandished the same type of weapon that killed Miller.

The other had seen a girl he described as "disturbed" and "crazy" because, for no reason, she'd tried to violently attack him. If these two accounts didn't supply evidence, as well as a motive, then nothing did. For it was pretty clear to Dr. Bright that Holland Santos and Lincoln Clark had eluded a deadly storm that wouldn't calm down until it killed someone. And Dr. Bright wasn't buying the story that these witnesses had simply popped up after Dawn's plea bargain was set. In fact, he remembered that back in May, the papers had said something about the early evening altercation in the convenience store, and he was positive authorities had known about her romp in Carl Schurz Park. So, it really bothered him that, for some reason, the testimonies of these "surprise" witnesses had been suppressed until now.

"Park Corpse Pictures Shock Court—Jurors grimaced and one wept yesterday when shown photos of the mutilated corpse of Mickey Miller after it was dragged from a lake in Central Park." As Dr. Bright read on about "deep lacerations, gaping wounds, severed hands, and a missing lower lip," his mind traveled back to those pictures that Detective Kelly had spread out on his desk. The wavy black hair strewn with leaves, the yellow balloon escaping from one eye, the organs swimming out of multiple holes, and the hand that looked like a half-eaten sandwich. And a question that had been nagging at Dr. Bright entered his mind again—how could anyone be tried for manslaughter in a case like this? A man was slaughtered, yes. But, technically, the term manslaughter meant "without intent to kill." How could anyone think this was done unintentionally after reading the description of the victim's body? It was these kinds of glaring contradictions, like the one entrenched in the final paragraph of the article, that utterly vexed Dr. Bright: "Dawn Fontaine, who pled guilty to manslaughter, meaning she didn't intend to kill, told authorities she 'hoped to cut off the victim's face and head so he wouldn't be recognized.'" Okay, so Dawn, thought Dr. Bright, the one who pled guilty to manslaughter, meaning she didn't intend to kill, told authorities she'd hoped to cut off the victim's face and head. He wondered if it could be possible that he was the only person who had noticed the egregious contradiction.

18

Dr. Bright hadn't noticed the Christmas decorations that adorned the Upper East Side until he saw an employee dismantling a display of Rudolph pulling Santa's sleigh in a department store window. Seeing the reindeer pulling the old elf's buggy through a starlit sky reminded him of a holiday tradition—years ago, he and Zoe would watch the cartoon on Christmas Eve and then wait to see Rudolph's red nose blinking in the night sky. The flickering glow was, of course, the aircraft warning light on top of the Chrysler Building, but Zoe didn't know that, and as soon as she saw it, she'd run down the hall and hop in bed. After soaking in the fond memory for a moment, Dr. Bright forced himself to reflect on this year's holiday. Zoe had planned to land in New York City, stay a few days with her father, and then spend Christmas with her mother in Buffalo, but she'd met an engineering major named Bruce who had invited her to spend the holiday with his family in California, and she'd accepted his invitation. Dr. Bright didn't blame her for her decision. For, he reasoned, anyone who would choose Buffalo over the West Coast would have to be insane. Nevertheless, it did mean that he'd be spending the holiday alone but considering the unbelievably stressful and tragic and circumstances of the past year, a little solitude seemed appealing.

∾

"Bombshell DNA Evidence a Blow to Baby-Face Butcher." As Dr. Bright read through a newspaper article, he learned that investigators had been working on scientifically linking Zander to the murder.

> *Blood consistent with the sixteen-year-old murder defendant and the grotesquely mutilated victim was commingled on the blade of a black folding knife believed to be the murder weapon. Prosecutors contend Zander Lee stabbed the forty-three-year-old Miller to death, then cut himself as he tried to saw off Miller's hands so the body couldn't be fingerprinted.*

Because the article was small, these words were squeezed into a frame around Zander's face, and there was something eerie about the damaging print surrounding his picture. It was almost as if the words formed a noose that was slowly tightening around the boy's neck. "Zander Lee faces a maximum sentence of ten years to life in prison if convicted of killing Miller." This last sentence closed like an iron door and Zander seemed trapped in the photograph forever. Dr. Bright pictured Sharon reading the article on this dark winter morning, and his heart broke for her. Coincidentally, after playing phone-tag for what seemed an eternity, Dr. Bright and Sharon had finally spoken last week. He had expected their conversation to retain some of the tender feelings they had shared before the murder, but he was mistaken—Sharon was polite and warm, but the intimacy in her voice was gone, and he knew that their budding romance had died. After thanking him several times for supporting Zander, she asked for some documents she needed for her insurance company and requested a meeting so she could retrieve them. Dr. Bright had offered to mail the documents, but she had insisted on meeting, and he knew that she wanted to say goodbye.

Later that day on the Upper East Side, Dr. Bright saw Sharon from across Second Avenue. She was sitting at a table by the window in the restaurant where they had agreed to meet. Because of the hopelessly dark winter sky and the candle lit on her table, she seemed illuminated and separate from the rest of the day. She looked even more ethereal inside the restaurant because the dreary day had painted the windows black, and hers was the only candle lit in an otherwise ashen room. Her eyes seemed fixated on something outside, but all Dr. Bright could discern were people passing, and he felt as if he were approaching a widow at a wake.

"Oh, hello," she said, her eyes rolling up to meet his.

"Sorry I'm late," he said, and after giving an embellished account of his commute, he handed her the documents she had requested.

"Won't you sit down?" She pointed to the empty chair at her table.

"Oh yes." While taking his seat he bumped into the table and spilled her water. "Shit! Sorry."

"Are you okay?" Sharon asked.

"Yes," he said, frantically trying to wipe up the mess.

"You don't have to be so nervous. I'm okay," she offered.

"Oh, I'm not nervous, I…" When he stopped wiping and their eyes met, she pierced him with an incredulous look.

Somewhat surprised, and rather embarrassed, he asked, "How could you tell I was nervous, Sharon?"

"How could I tell?" She laughed. "You come in here talking thirty miles an hour about traffic, and then forget to sit down." Her pretty laugh let him know that she wasn't offended.

Sharon spent the first half hour convincing Dr. Bright that she was all right, but he got the distinct impression she was also trying to convince herself of this. She did look better than she had the last time they had met on Zander's birthday—her skin was more vibrant, and her eyes were no longer red. Yet, there was a fragile quality to her voice that belied her sturdy demeanor. She was seeing a psychologist, she explained, who had been helping her see that she was using Zander's crime as a way of "crucifying herself." Then, she told Dr. Bright some very disturbing things about her ex-husband, Jack, who had simply "cut Zander out of his life." Not only had Jack never visited his son in jail, but he'd also never even called or written to find out how the boy was doing. This kind of neglect was nothing new, and Sharon had even diagnosed Zander's "nonexistent" father.

"Well, I'm not a psychologist or anything, but if there is such a thing as a pathological liar, then that's what Jack is. And he was like an onion, you know? Peel away one lie, and there's another. And another. And another. Layer after layer of stupid lies. Lies, lies, lies. An endless amount. But I didn't see the full harm in it until Zander was born. He'd lie right to the kid's face. Tell him he'd take him to this place or that, and then, of course, he never would."

Here their waiter interrupted, so they each ordered a salad just to get rid of him.

"So, you were saying your ex-husband was a liar…"

"Worse. He lied, cheated, drank, did drugs. And, like a lot of naïve young brides, I thought he'd change his ways, but he never did." She took a deep breath and looked out the window for a moment.

"Drinking and drugs, huh?" Dr. Bright asked.

"Oh yeah, and that's what finally did it. I told him if he ever brought drugs back into the house again, I'd divorce him."

The doctor added, "And he brought them home again, I take it."

"Yes, several times. But one morning when Zander was around three years old, I heard him crying upstairs. He'd found Jack's cocaine stash and thought it was sugar. Oh Doctor, you can't imagine what it's like for a mother to see her baby holding a bag of cocaine, and, of course, I was horrified, because I didn't know if he'd ingested it or what. But I didn't want to call an ambulance because I thought there might be cops, and then it hit me. Here I was, feeling like a criminal, like it was my cocaine, and I realized what a lie I'd been living."

"So you called the ambulance?" Dr. Bright asked.

Sharon answered, "Oh yeah, and the police, too. Because in that split second I'd actually considered endangering my baby's life to hide my husband's addiction." She cringed as though the whole thing was happening again. "Poor kid. I'll never forget those screams. He kept on yelling, 'Fire, fire!' because some of that crap got in his eye."

"Jesus," the doctor said with a sigh.

"And they told me it really could've damaged his vision if I hadn't called right away. And all I kept thinking about was that split second I had hesitated… that split second where hiding Jack's drug problem was more important to me than Zander's safety. I'll never forgive myself for that."

"Yes, but everything turned out okay," Dr. Bright said.

"Did it?" she asked, alluding to Zander's crime.

"Yeah, but Sharon, that morning has nothing to do with…"

"Really?" she remarked with palpable skepticism. "I'm not so sure about that, Doctor."

"What do you mean?"

"Well, that day I was fortunate enough to catch myself compromising Zander's well-being, but how many times had it happened before, and how many times has it happened since? See, Doctor, I'll never forget that split second… I was so lost… it was like driving through a blizzard without windshield wipers… and I literally had to force myself to call the ambulance."

"But you did call," he affirmed.

"Yes, that time, but how many times did I stay lost in that blizzard when Zander needed me?" Her moist eyes shined in the candlelight. "That's the thing that really bothers me, and because it was all unconscious, 'a zone of forgetfulness,' to quote my therapist, I have no way of knowing." She wiped her eyes and straightened up when their waiter set down their salads and walked away.

"Listen …"

The waiter spun around because he thought Dr. Bright was talking to him but evaporated when he heard the doctor's next sentence.

"I think you're still trying to crucify yourself."

"You do?" She looked vacantly at her salad.

"Yes. Look, I can't begin to imagine what you're going through. It must be pure hell, but you've got to stop blaming yourself."

"I can't stop," she whispered, so delicately her words seemed to break apart in the air.

"It's not a question of can or can't. You *have to*, for your own emotional survival. You have to stop torturing yourself with these lies."

"Lies?" she asked blankly.

"Yes, lies. I don't really know exactly what happened that night in the park, and I doubt anyone ever will. But I do know that your moment of hesitation when Zander was little, or a mountain of those moments, doesn't account for his actions that night."

Tears flew out of her eyes.

"And I'll tell you another thing, Sharon. I know you two have had your problems, but Zander loves you and he knows you love him."

Here she looked at Dr. Bright with such pleading, vulnerable eyes that he almost couldn't return her gaze. But somehow, he summoned the strength to look into her eyes. In this hour of forgiveness, they were both receiving grace.

19

Even though the meeting with Sharon had been a sad goodbye, the encounter had stitched up a wound in his heart, and he realized he needed the same type of closure with Dawn's family. So, when Howard neglected to return his phone calls, he decided to stalk him. Yes, Dr. Bright, a professional psychologist, an intelligent man who flew the flag of emotional well-being, decided to stalk someone. He'd even had a little fun in the planning of this clandestine affair. He had put together a camouflage outfit, mostly browns and grays to match a lifeless December morning. Then, he'd set his alarm clock for five a.m., and was out the door by six.

The Fontaines' building stood in total darkness, and it occurred to Dr. Bright that he might have scheduled this mission a little too early. The only people awake on the Upper East Side of Manhattan at six a.m. were bus drivers, cops, and nannies getting someone else's kids ready for school. He bought a newspaper and a coffee and went to Central Park, but the sky hadn't filled with light yet, so he sat on a bench just outside the park next to a lamp post.

"Baby-Face Butcher Tells Cops She Used LSD with Slay Victim—The teenage girl who admitted participating in the 'Baby-Face Butcher' attack on a man in Central Park told cops the victim turned her onto LSD weeks before the killing." Despite Zander's promises that hard-core drugs hadn't played a role in the crime, Dr. Bright had harbored doubts, and this article confirmed his suspicions. And, while looking across Fifth Avenue, it occurred to him that his two teenage clients had crossed this very street covered in Mickey Miller's blood a year ago.

After two hours, his hopes of catching Howard had faded. Besides, he really needed more caffeine. Fortunately for Dr. Bright, there happened to be a coffee stand on the corner of Eighty-sixth and Fifth. The only problem was that a guy wearing a hoodie had just handed over a bunch of change, which the vendor was now slowly counting. After several failed attempts to get the vendor's attention, Dr. Bright, now out of patience, demanded a cup of coffee.

The vendor quickly looked up, then continued to lethargically count the change, and though the hooded customer didn't say anything, Dr. Bright felt his eyes on him. While considering his other coffee options, the doctor was startled by the vendor shouting, "My friend! My friend! You money! You money!" And turning around, he saw the hooded man hurriedly walking away. Dr. Bright impulsively snatched the two dollar bills out of the vendor's hand and started running after the fleeing man who happened to be covering a lot of ground with his quick, truncated strides. In fact, he looked like he might've stolen something by the way he was weaving through people. At the corner of Eighty-fourth Street, Dr. Bright finally caught up with him.

"Sir! Sir!" Dr. Bright exclaimed. "You forgot your money!"

The man continued taking choppy strides, but when the doctor put his hand on his shoulder, he stopped. The hooded fugitive was Howard Fontaine.

"Doctor… Doctor… I…" he said, looking at the sidewalk, "… I've been meaning to call you… I haven't had a minute."

The doctor placed the money in Howard's palm. "Do you have a minute now?"

"Well…" Howard looked at his watch. "I have several appointments…"

"Please," Dr. Bright implored him, "all I'm asking for is ten minutes. Do you think you could grant me that?"

And here the walls within Howard's eyes crumbled. "Sure, I've got some time. Come on."

They walked into the building that Dr. Bright had been watching for the past two hours. After the elevator lifted them in the palm of its creamy hand, they walked down the same mauve hallway Dr. Bright had walked down on Thanksgiving morning a little over a year ago. As Howard's key disappeared into the lock, the doctor asked if the visit would bother Louisa. The question seemed to knock Howard unconscious because his head and hands suddenly dangled to the floor. Then, after a few moments, he raised his head and said in a defeated voice, "Louisa's not here." Sensing that further inquiry would be painful, Dr. Bright abandoned the subject.

With Herculean effort, Howard opened the door, and everything Dr. Bright had expected to see, including the gold coffee table shaped like a fish, was gone. In fact, the apartment was completely empty, except for some crates, a refrigerator without a door, and a piece of sunlight shaped like an angel on the floor.

"Moving," Howard said listlessly. "Don't need this place anymore."

Dr. Bright considered asking Howard why they were moving but it was clear that his daughter's actions and the invasive media had made the city uninhabitable.

"We have to sit on these," he pointed to some cardboard boxes, "because the furniture left yesterday." It was interesting that Howard said the furniture "left," as though it had gone of its own volition, as if it was just another thing in his life that he couldn't control. When directed to sit on a box marked "Fragile," Dr. Bright protested, but Howard assured him he had written that on all of them. However, the second the doctor sat down, a snap, followed by two bursting sounds, filled the empty apartment, and the look on Howard's face suggested it must have been his heart in there.

"Howard, I'm sorry," Dr. Bright said, standing.

"It's okay, it's okay." He waved him back down. "I was going to throw out most of that stuff anyway."

Dr. Bright hesitantly sat back down. But the second he rested his weight, two more bursts, like lamps hurled against a wall, filled the tragic room. Howard immediately raised a hand to thwart an apology. Then he pulled a handkerchief out of his pocket and looked around. "Funny how a home can disappear in a day."

"Disappear?" Dr. Bright asked.

"Yesterday, this was my home. Today, I don't recognize it," Howard said, and started picking at the tape on his box with a fingernail. By the way he was immersed in this task, Dr. Bright could tell this seemingly mindless action was deeply symbolic. It was almost as if his happiness was packed inside those boxes, and if he could remove the tape, he could have his happiness back.

Dr. Bright said, "I know this is a tough time, but I was hoping you and I could talk about everything that happened."

"Everything that happened?" Howard's question was more like an echo than an inquiry.

"Yes... see... we... you and I, that is, haven't spoken since the arrest..."

Howard finally managed to extricate a tiny corner of the tape.

"And," Dr. Bright continued, hoping to broach the subject of the lawsuit, "there's probably a lot of resentment and blame."

Howard pulled at the corner of the tape, making a violent ripping sound. "Blame?" He stopped pulling. "Yes, there's been a lot of blame."

"Well, I think we should talk about it, don't you?"

"Doctor." He ripped the tape the rest of the way and it fell to the floor like a dead snake. "This is very nice of you, but I think your work here is done."

"But you said you blamed me for things, which I totally understand."

When Howard took off his glasses to wipe them, his eyes got really small. "I don't blame you, Doctor."

"You don't?"

Howard's eyes swam around like big blue fish when the glasses returned to his face. "Doctor," he said, picking at another piece of tape on the box, "do you want to know what ruined *Louisa's* life? Blame." He violently ripped off the tape like he was tearing the skin off a dead animal. "It was like she was taken over by some kind of ravenous wolf, and once it ate everything inside her, it started eating me and Dawn." He looked down and suddenly smiled. "I'm gonna miss that."

"What?" the doctor inquired.

"The light here… so beautiful. See the way it spreads?" Howard gazed at the luminous angel on the floor. "By ten o'clock, she'll be over there," he said, pointing towards Dawn's room and smiling, as though he could already see its golden wings spreading on his daughter's door. "Poor girl never had a chance. Louisa blamed her for everything… when she first came to us, Louisa was like a kid with a new toy, but after that first month or so, she just got sick of Dawn, refused to pick her up, wouldn't even look at her… and the kid knew, she knew…" His hand slowly fell to his side. "Kid used to look up at me with those big blue eyes… that's all she was at first."

"All she was?" Dr. Bright asked.

"Yeah, Dawn," he said, smiling again, "the runt… that's what I used to call her. She was born prematurely you know, only four and a half pounds, about the size of a doll. She had these big blue eyes, bigger than mine," he said. His hand slowly raised again. "There was something about them though, they weren't filled with wonder like most baby's eyes, they seemed older and kind of fragile, like they'd already seen too much, and she was only a few months old." His hand dropped to his side again. "And she never cried, never. Doctor, did you ever hear of a baby not crying?"

Dr. Bright didn't answer, because Howard wasn't really talking to him.

"I mean, never, never at night, never when she was sick, not even when Louisa wouldn't pick her up." He took off his glasses and cleaned them again, perhaps hoping that when he put them back on the world would be different. "She never picked her up, not after that first month. That's pretty tragic, isn't it?"

"Yes, Howard, it's very sad."

"I used to come home from work, and they'd be sitting across from one another in the living room like two adults… Louisa with that big scowl on her face and Daw…" The last letter of her name got caught in his throat, but he swallowed it and continued, "She was so damn small, Doc, I used to call her the runt; she was like a tiny doll, and there'd be these huge blue eyes staring at me from her baby blanket. Oh, but those eyes, they were like two skies shining on me whenever I came home, they shined the way Louisa's used to… and that was the weird thing…"

"What was weird, Howard?"

Suddenly, out of nowhere, Howard burst out laughing. "One time, I shouldn't laugh, but one time, in a state of delirium, during one of her nine hundred nervous breakdowns, Louisa was in the bed deliriously screaming that Dawn had stolen her soul." His laughter subsided. "She was rocking back and forth on the bed like that girl in *The Exorcist*. So, of course, Lowenstein prescribed Valium, her first drug." His bright tone blackened. "That's when I lost her, you know. She never came back from the drugs." He stared down at the floor for what seemed to be the length of a summer day. And when he finally spoke, his words were, "If Lowenstein had just talked with her, he would've found out what I already knew… I mean it was so fucking clear…"

"What was clear, Howard?"

"That all this depression stuff was bullshit… Louisa was jealous of Dawn, she hated her, and she was screaming so the poor kid would know it. You should've heard the things she said: 'She's not mine! I don't want her! Send her back! Send her back!' And," he said, indicating with a wave of his hand the proximity of their bedrooms, "isn't it obvious she wanted the kid to hear it?"

"Was Dawn old enough to understand?" Dr. Bright asked softly.

"Old enough to understand what?" Howard queried.

"That Louisa didn't want her?"

"How old do you have to be for that, Doctor?"

The psychologist lowered his eyes.

"Plus, this didn't just happen once. The time I'm talking about happened when Dawn was around six months old, but Louisa spit out that kind of bile all throughout Dawn's life."

"You mean, she said that kind of stuff when Dawn was older?" Dr. Bright asked.

"Yelled it! Yelled it! Yelled it!" He got up and started pacing around the room. "All the fucking time! But always in the convenient clutches of some delirium… and always the next day it was, 'What did I say? What did I say?' Fucking bitch." He stopped and stared at an empty wall. "I suppose I shouldn't say that, because who really knows?"

"Who knows what, Howard?"

"What's going on inside someone else. Barely know what's going on inside myself." With his hands dangling down to his knees and his head tilted to one side, Howard looked like an unattended puppet. "Doctor," his head quickly rose as though the puppeteer had just come back, "even if she was suffering from some kind of depression and feeling that stuff inside, did she have to scream it at the kid? I mean, it's one thing to feel it, but did she have to make the kid suffer, too?"

"Well, I…"

"Dawn didn't ask to be brought here. There were plenty of other mothers who wanted her, really wanted her, but I had connections, so… it just makes me sick to think of how much better off she might've been. And then, there was a time when we decided to let someone else have her, someone who could really care for her. So we contacted the adoption agency and explained the situation." Howard put both of his hands on the wall like he was being frisked.

"So, what happened?" the doctor inquired.

"I went into her bedroom early the following morning to take her back to the agency... real early... still dark... guess I was hoping she'd be asleep, but when I picked her up..." He took his hands off the wall and looked at them.

"What Howard? What happened?" Dr. Bright asked.

He slowly turned around. "She said her first word."

"What did she say?"

"She said 'day?'" Two tears slipped down his cheeks. "This little voice in the darkness inquiring so succinctly... and when I turned on the light her big blue eyes were shining up at me and she was smiling so brightly. I knew at that moment she was my daughter, that she'd always be my daughter, and that no one would ever take her away from me." He stopped, closed his eyes, and said quietly, "But I guess they took her away, didn't they?" He leaned against the wall.

"Yes, but she won't be gone forever," the doctor said.

"Gone?" Howard looked up at Dr. Bright, then quickly looked back down. "That's not what I meant." He bent his knees and slowly began sliding down the wall. "Think I'd like to be alone now, Doctor."

"Okay." Dr. Bright rose just as the distraught man finished his descent to the floor. "Call me if you need anything, okay?"

Howard didn't respond, and the doctor let himself out. However, before closing the door, Dr. Bright glanced at the broken man sitting among scattered boxes. Happiness is a delicate fabric that can be torn apart at a moment's notice.

20

A brutally cold and dark winter held New York in its icy hands for five long months, and when snowplows had to clear the streets for the Saint Patrick's Day Parade, people began to wonder if it would ever leave. However, by April, the chill began to recede, and many called it a miracle when temperatures climbed into the fifties on Easter Sunday. After that, spring apologized for her tardiness by putting on a glorious display—cherry blossoms painted Central Park pink, buttercups bloomed all over the Bronx, daffodils burst along the Henry Hudson Parkway, and tulips brightened the Park Avenue malls.

While cleaning up the waiting room outside his office on an afternoon in May, Dr. Bright came across a newspaper someone had left behind that had signaled the end of the "Baby-Faced Butchers" case back in February. Even though he had read the article three months ago, he sat down and perused it once more.

Baby-Face Butcher Gets Ten Years—Ending a horrific case that stunned the city with a mixture of cruelty, wealth, and drunkenness, the visibly frustrated judge recommended Lee not be paroled for ten years. A night that began with a beer party in Strawberry Fields ended with Miller's mutilated body being dumped in Central Park Lake after Lee, incensed with jealous rage, stabbed Miller over thirty times, then tried to cut his head off.

Again, Dr. Bright found the eerie pastiche of pictures—the profile of Zander in the courtroom with closed eyes next to a snapshot of Mickey Miller's smiling face, and because the man's face was tilted to the left, it almost seemed to be resting on the boy's shoulder. Equally eerie was the photograph of Dawn hovering above the other two like a sinless angel. But the most bizarre component of the article was the jury's decision to convict Zander of manslaughter because it meant that both suspects had been found guilty of *unintentionally* murdering Mickey Miller. Even though the teens had stabbed him over thirty-six times, tried to cut off his face and hands, and had dumped what was left of his body into Central Park Lake, the killing had been ruled inadvertent. And the reason for this mishandling of justice? Jurors said they "could not be 100 percent positive Zander committed the murder." Some said they felt "Dawn was the real murderer," but because her plea bargain guaranteed she didn't have to testify, they "didn't get the opportunity to judge her." So, in a sense, jurors had declared it a stalemate in which no one really lost, except for Mickey Miller, who had lost his life.

Dr. Bright was mortified when the sad irony of his situation occurred to him—here he was reading a newspaper from February because he hadn't come to terms with the catastrophe caused by his clients and he was, in a sense, stuck. Like a dead leaf glued to the ground, he had been watching the progress of others without being able to move himself—Brenda Fixx had recognized the untenable nature of a sunglasses store in Manhattan where it rained and snowed half the year and had moved her shop to Miami; Brad had realized that his fiancée had been the problem, not his penis; for, on a trip to Santa Barbara she had complained the entire time about their accommodations (they were staying in the Spanish Garden, a four-star hotel, not the Belmond, a five-star hotel), and it had occurred to Brad that she was just a spoiled bitch and he called off the wedding. Furthermore, the Fontaines had moved to Connecticut, and because he hadn't received a summons, he knew they had dropped the bogus lawsuit against him and had begun to move on with their lives. However, as Dr. Bright recalled a session with Evelyn around Valentine's Day, he realized that the most astounding progress had been made by her—she had come into his office overflowing with joy because she and Alex had fallen in love.

"Didn't even know we were dating, did you, Doctor?" she had asked with a triumphant smile.

"No, I didn't, Evelyn," he admitted.

"Anyway, he's got his issues, but I'll take a real guy with flaws over those fake guys I used to invent."

Her last sentence had hit him like a left hook because she'd just revealed her darkest secret so dispassionately.

"I just surprised you, didn't I?" She laughed. "You look like you just saw a spaceship."

"Well, I guess I am a little surprised," he said, rubbing his eyes.

Evelyn continued. "I mean, I know you knew all along. And after a while, I did, too. But we never spoke about it."

"Right, right," he said, still stunned by her acknowledgement.

"But do you want to know the reason I can talk about that stuff now?" She pointed her finger at him and with shimmering eyes, spoke delicately, *"You. You, you, you."* And the pronoun seemed to make her sad, because each time it was repeated a little tear fell from her eyes. *"You were the only therapist who ever respected me, who ever made me feel safe."*

When she wiped her eyes, Dr. Bright handed her a tissue.

"I always knew you were on my side, no matter what," Evelyn continued. *"Even if I talked about crazy shit like imaginary men, you never judged me. And you know something, Doctor? If it weren't for you, I never would've talked about those imaginary men, and talking about them made them fade... because when they were kept inside they were powerful, but once they were thrown into the light, they were weak... know what I mean? Kind of like vampires."*

"Vampires?" he asked.

"Yeah," she replied. *"You know how vampires have to stay in their coffins during the day because the sunlight kills them?"*

"So, you were keeping those vampires hidden?" Dr. Bright queried.

"Yeah, that's exactly what those imaginary men were, vampires, but because my past therapists were so judgmental and intimidating, those vampires could stay in their coffins and prey on me at night."

The conversation with Evelyn faded from his mind when the phone in his office rang, and after folding the old newspaper, he got up and answered it.

"Hello?" Dr. Bright said.

"What's up, Doc?"

Fear swept through the doctor's mind because the voice on the other line sounded like Zander's, and he feared that his mental choo-choo train had finally gone around the bend. However, to test his grim suspicions, he decided to ask the caller a question

"Is this Zander?" he asked.

"No, it's fuckin' Santa Claus. Course it's Zander, who'd ja think?"

Because the brash, cynical tone laden with teenage angst couldn't belong to anyone other than the imprisoned teen, Dr. Bright joyfully exclaimed, "Zander!"

"You alright, Doc?" the boy asked.

"Of course, I'm all right, why?"

"Well, you sound like you was in the middle a somethin'… like maybe you was bangin' some broad when I called."

"No, Zander," the doctor rejoined. "I wasn't in the middle of anything. I'm just surprised and glad to hear from you, that's all."

"Are ya sure?" The boy replied. "'Cuz I could call ya back after the hottie leaves."

"No, Zander, there isn't any hottie. How are you?"

"Well, I'm up in this fuckin' place, so I'm not exactly awesome," he said, referring to the prison in Upstate New York.

"You sound like you're doing okay," Dr. Bright said, hoping this was true.

"Yeah, well, up here you don't really do okay or not okay. You just kinda exist. Like, every day they tell you what to do, and every day it's the same thing. It's not like you're really livin'."

"I see what you mean," Dr. Bright said.

Zander continued, "It's like you're the broom and they're sweeping. 'Cept in bed at night. That's the only time I'm not a broom, cause they tell me to sleep, but I don't sleep. So that's the only time they're not pushin' me around."

"You don't sleep?" Dr. Bright asked, knowing the extreme effects that lack of sleep can have on people.

Zander answered. "Can't. But up here, you don't really need to sleep, cause you're just lyin' around mosta the time."

"Well, do you ever nap in the afternoon?" the doctor asked, hoping it was a possibility.

"Ah, ya know, sometimes. Couple minutes here and there. It's like my body's tired, but my brain ain't."

"You mean your thoughts are keeping you awake?"

"Yeah, sometimes, Doc, but it's like they're not my thoughts. Like they're in my head, but they're not mine. Sounds stupid, but sometimes I think, like, maybe the dude who had my cell last left a few memories lyin' around. Crazy, right?"

"No, Zander, that's not crazy." Dr. Bright believed that Zander was haunted by his own demons and by the dark cloud of torment hovering over all of the other lost souls in that place.

"Yeah, but Doc, people don't leave thoughts lyin' around like coins in a couch."

"No, Zander, they don't, but that's a perfect way to describe the sensation of subconscious thoughts... the thoughts you're not ready to accept... consciously."

"Yeah, I see what you're sayin', but some of the thoughts are so wack. Like some of 'em don't make any sense at all."

"Give me an example," the doctor urged.

Zander said that last week he'd been on his cot reading *Hot Rod,* and then "out of nowhere," he imagined himself dragging garbage bags into an alley he'd never seen before. Suddenly all sorts of "nasty shit" had started spilling out of the bags, and Zander was standing in a puddle. The "wack" thing about the puddle was that it had been the only thing in the daydream void of color. There had been a gray alley, green garbage bags, and a sliver of blue sky above him. But the puddle spreading at his feet had been black and white "like in old movies." Dr. Bright explained that clearly this was a subconscious vision depicting Zander's fading denial. The garbage bags represented the guilt he was trying to throw away, and the contents spilling out of them were those feelings refusing to be discarded. The growing puddle was colorless because he hadn't fully accepted those feelings. But, the contrasting hues indicated that he did recognize the feelings, which was extremely positive.

The second daydream Zander told Dr. Bright about was loosely based on the movie *Jaws*, which he'd watched on TV several weeks before the murder. Once again, he had been reading in bed when, without warning, he was aboard the *Orca* chasing a giant shark. He "kept pumpin' harpoons into the big bastard," but the shark "kept pulling the barrels down." And when all the barrels were gone, Zander found himself alone on the stern.

The meaning of this vision, like the others, seemed obvious to the doctor. Water in dreams, as any freshman in Psych 101 learns, represents the unconscious, and clearly the boy was probing this mysterious realm. When Dr. Bright explained the symbolic components of the vision and how positive it was, Zander perceptively asked, "Well, if it was so positive then why didn't the barrels come back up?" Rather than answering this, Dr. Bright asked him what he'd been thinking about while he was alone on the stern. Zander reluctantly said that he'd been thinking of his mom. He'd pictured her on a bench on the Upper East Side of Manhattan at Carl Schurtz Park eating an ice cream cone during a summer long ago. And he'd seen her face in the audience when he played a carrot in an elementary school play. The last memory had been her disconsolate expression as police handcuffed him on the morning of the murder.

"Them memories of my mom were the barrels comin' back up, weren't they, Doc?"

Dr. Bright didn't say a word, because Zander already knew the answer to his question was yes. With the confidence that comes from emotional clarity, Zander finally said how badly he felt about the crime's impact on his mom. He even said, "It's like I murdered her that night." When Dr. Bright asked him to elaborate on that topic, Zander explained:

"Fuckin' son's a murderer, papers been comparin' me with Jeffrey Dahmer, my fuckin' picture's plastered everywhere, and for a long time they were talkin' life sentence. Imagine that, Doc. Her son's only seventeen and they're already talkin' about takin' him away forever. And my father's a fuckin' joke, wouldn't even help her with the lawyer's fees, and those bastards took every cent she had. Fuckin' had to sell our apartment. Lives in this little shithole now, and she fuckin' loved that place."

"Well, Zander, if she had to do it all over again, I'm sure she'd do it the same way. And if those lawyers helped reduce your sentence, then I'm sure things like the apartment don't really matter to her."

In the silence, Dr. Bright heard choppy breathing and he knew Zander was fighting tears. Yet, this imperfect quiet was torn in half by a racket as startling as shrieks in the dead of night.

"What was that?" the doctor asked.

"Hold on a sec, Doc."

As if the boy accidentally dropped the phone into a tub filled with water, the banging sounds ceased and muffled voices emerged.

"Hey, I gotta get going," Zander said after a brief pause.

"Zander, what was that noise?"

"Ah, just this big prick lettin' me know my time was up."

"But what was that banging?" the doctor probed.

"Him hittin' the door with his nightstick. That's how the guards communicate with us. Kinda like killin' two birds with one stone."

"What do you mean, Zander?"

"Well, he's reminding me my time is up, but he's also reminding me he's got that stick. Plus, they talk to you as little as possible, cause talkin's for people in society, and we're not fit for society, so talkin's too good for us. But, Doc, the reason I called you is they got this mandatory counseling I gotta do… but the thing is, the shrinks up here are a bunch a losers."

"They're losers?" Dr. Bright asked.

"Fuckin' dregs of society, man. Fuckin' drag 'em in off bar stools. This one fuckin' guy smelled so much like liquor, I almost got drunk off his breath. Most of 'em are clowns from the college in town."

"Oh, so you mean they're interns," Dr. Bright tried to clarify.

"Yeah, yeah, interns. Just a fancy way a sayin' student, right?"

"Yes, Zander," the doctor laughed at the boy's precocious comment, "that's right."

"And they're all really fuckin' young. This dude the other day had more zits than me. And, Doc, I mean, if you needed an operation you wouldn't want some student cuttin' you open, would ja? You'd want a doctor, right? Some dude with an ad in the yellow pages and diplomas on his walls, right?"

"Right," Dr. Bright agreed.

"And I feel like I got a lot a' shit going on right now… you know like with my subconscious… and I don't feel like talking to Bart Simpson about it."

"I hear you, Zander."

"Anyway, they said I could talk to you if you wanted to come up here."

Zander's request startled Dr. Bright. However, the request wasn't as unexpected as the happiness it instantly brought the man—his heart burst with joy like a pinata and colorful candies flew everywhere. But Zander mistook the doctor's silence as rejection.

"They even said we could do it over the phone, if coming here was a pain. But it's cool if you don't want to."

"No, no, Zander, it's not that," Dr. Bright said. "But I don't think phone sessions would work."

"Yeah, I hear ya," the boy said, his voice as gray as a winter sky. "Just thought I'd ask."

"But I would definitely be willing to come up there."

"You would?!" Zander shouted ebulliently. But then, as if suspicious of his own happiness, he repeated the question in a tone more endemic to prison life. "You would?"

"Of course, I would."

"Cool!" the teen exclaimed, his joy rebelling again. "There's a train that comes right into town, and there's a shuttle to the prison… my mom does it every week, super easy and…"

Three more growls from the guard's nightstick shattered the rest of Zander's words.

"So look, Doc, is it a deal?"

"Yes, Zander, it's a deal."

"Awesome. Could ya do Friday afternoons?"

"Well, I'll have to look at my schedule but I think Fridays will work."

"Cool… listen, I really appreciate this and… hey, hold on a second." The phone dropped and there was a succession of squeaking sounds. "Okay, I'm back. That prick just went outside for a cigarette, so I got a few more seconds."

"Can you see him from where you're sitting, Zander?"

"Nah, but I can see his smoke," he said, and perhaps because their business was somewhat concluded for now, a silence descended. Just as Dr. Bright was getting ready to speak, the guard's nightstick shattered the quiet again.

"Doc, I gotta go… see ya Friday!"

21

As Dr. Bright crossed the Triborough Bridge at sunset, Manhattan began rising unexpectedly out of the sea like long-submerged Atlantis. Starting low on the horizon, the city surged northward like an enormous wave gathering strength and size before reaching its precarious crest in Midtown. When his car got stuck in the swamp of commuters on FDR Drive, the doctor reflected upon his session with Zander hours before at the Westchester County Jail. Although the accommodations were grim, the boy looked better than he ever had—the rage in his eyes had dissolved, and the bite in his tone had softened because he was finally engaged in the process of healing. Near the end of their conversation, Zander had asked an unexpected question:

"Do you believe in God, Doc?"

"Yes, Zander. I do," the doctor responded. *"How about you?"*

"I ain't so sure, but I'm in big fuckin' trouble if He does exist."

"What do you mean?" Dr. Bright asked.

"'Cuz if this seems bad now," Zander indicated the prison with a wave of his hand, "then I'm scared to think what the big guy has in store for me later."

"I wouldn't worry too much about later," Dr. Bright said. "Just concern yourself with now."

"Yeah, but what about Hell? With them boiling rivers of blood and those bad-ass demons with pitchforks?"

"Well, that's up to you, Zander," Dr. Bright replied.

"What do ya mean it's 'up to me'?" The boy asked, bewildered by the doctor's response.

"Bloody rivers and demons are manifestations of guilt. When you forgive yourself, they'll go away."

"So, like you're saying that Hell only exists in people's brains?"

"Yes, Zander. That's what I'm saying."

"So, it's not real?"

"Oh, no," the doctor replied. "It's very real."

"But only in my mind?"

"That's right."

"But what if I can't forgive myself?" the boy asked as clouds gathered in his eyes.

"Forgiveness is a long process, Zander, and it takes a lot of work."

"Yeah, but…" two tears rolled down his cheeks. "I fuckin' killed a guy. How am I supposed to forgive myself for that?"

Five soft knocks on the door interrupted their conversation.

"What was that?" Dr. Bright asked.

"The guard," Zander wiped his face. "We have five minutes left."

"Doesn't use his nightstick anymore?" The doctor referred to the clamorous knocking he'd heard over the phone last week.

"Yeah, he does, but he knows you're here, so he won't. Prick."

"Well, anyway, Zander... forgiveness is a process, and it takes a long time."

"Well, I got lots of time." The boy looked around the beige conference room with hunched shoulders.

"That's right," Dr. Bright responded. "Time to reflect, heal, and forgive yourself."

"Hey, Doc!" He suddenly sat up. "I'll be twenty-six when I get out a' here."

"Yes, Zander," said Dr. Bright, doing the math in his mind. "That's right."

"Everything'll be different then, huh, Doc?" Zander stared at the ceiling with glazed eyes, as if the enormity of the lost decade had just occurred to him.

"Yes, Zander," the doctor said softly. "A lot of things will be different."

"Think they'll still have iPhones?" the boy asked absently.

"I'm not sure, Zander."

Their conversation ceased and for several moments the only sound was the ticking of the immutable clock.

"Hey, Doc," Zander said with a sudden sense of urgency, "they got this chapel here. You should check it out."

"Have you been going there?"

"Well, yeah. We get to go there for thirty minutes once a week, and it beats sitting in my stupid cell."

Another knock, followed by the sound of jingling keys, filled the small room.

"Anyway," the boy continued, "hang a left on the first floor after ya get outta the elevator. It's right before the drinking fountains. Will ya check it out?"

"Of course, I will."

"Promise?"

"Yes, Zander. I promise."

The door opened, and a guard entered. "Time's up, sir. Will you follow me, please?"

"Yes, of course." Dr. Bright stood up. "See you in two weeks, Zander."

"Thanks, Doc," the boy said, looking deeply into his therapist's eyes. "I really appreciate it."

"You're welcome."

"And don't forget to check out the chapel!" the boy shouted.

"I won't forget."

Dr. Bright had been delighted to see Zander's sojourn into spirituality. It meant that he was seeking spiritual salvation; and although the man wanted to get on the road to beat the traffic, he decided to honor the boy's request and visit the chapel. After getting off the elevator, he followed the signs and eventually came to a wooden door with a cross on it. The smell of incense and candles filled his nostrils as he entered the quaint chapel furnished with holy water, pews, a pulpit, and three stained glass windows covered by iron mesh. Dr. Bright noticed a woman kneeling near the altar, and although he wasn't a fan of formal worship, he sat down and prayed for the souls of Zander, Dawn, and Mickey Miller.

While he was meditating, he heard the woman in front gather her belongings and slowly walk down the aisle past him. When the door didn't open behind him, he assumed she was crossing herself with holy water, so he finished his prayer. However, when he turned to leave, he was surprised to see Sharon staring at him with illuminated eyes. Dr. Bright must have had a comical expression on his face because she started laughing and beckoned him to follow her out the door.

"Funny seeing you here, stranger," Sharon said with a coy smile when they were in the hallway together.

"Oh," he replied. "I've agreed to meet Zander twice a month for counseling. Didn't he tell you?"

"Yes," she responded. "He told me."

"Well, I hope it's okay… I just assumed…"

"It's more than okay," Sharon said, moving closer to him. "I meant it was funny seeing you in there." She pointed to the chapel.

"Oh… I like to pray sometimes," he said self-consciously.

"No, no, no." She laughed at him. "Seeing you in there on a Friday afternoon."

"Why?" Dr. Bright asked, now genuinely confused.

"Because I always go to the chapel on Fridays, before I visit Zander."

"Oh," said Dr. Bright, slowly connecting the dots. "I see."

Sharon looked deeply into his eyes. "Did Zander ask you to visit him on Friday afternoons?"

"Yes," he replied, blissfully helpless in her gaze.

"And did he ask you to visit the chapel?" She took another step toward him.

"Yes."

Sharon moved close enough for him to smell the perfume on her neck. "Are you sorry you came?"

"No."

When Dr. Bright went to embrace her, his arms had turned to stone and remained motionless at his sides. It was as if some spiritual veil made of the same impenetrable fabric that separates dreams from reality or life from death had fallen between them, and they were suddenly separated by a formidable chasm. He knew that Sharon felt it too because she had taken a step back, and the light in her eyes had dimmed.

"We can't do this," she said flatly.

"Yes, I know," Dr. Bright replied.

After a few moments of silence that felt like an eternity, Sharon said, "But it was sweet of Zander to try."

"Yes," he agreed.

"Kids don't always understand stuff like this," she continued. "They think because they want something to happen, it should happen. They don't think of things like priorities and timing."

Even though Sharon had appeared to be discussing the puerile perspective of teens, Dr. Bright knew she had actually been talking about their own dilemma—here were two adults that desperately wanted to be together whose romance had, ironically, been forever destroyed by the boy yearning for their union. For, when Zander murdered Mickey Miller, he had murdered their chance of love.

"Well, I better go up and see Zander," she said, looking at her watch.

"Can I walk you to the elevator?" Dr. Bright asked.

"Of course," she replied with manufactured enthusiasm, and they walked down the cavernous hallway together. When they reached the elevator, Sharon pressed the button, and after a moment of silence, said, "Thank you, again, for visiting Zander."

"It's my pleasure," the doctor rejoined.

Under normal circumstances, people with this much feeling for one another would have hugged before saying goodbye, but because there was no context for this situation, no scripted protocol, both had stood like mannequins in a store window. When the elevator arrived, Sharon stepped on and turned around, and surprisingly, her eyes that had been dimmed were filled with the tender light of affection, and Dr. Bright felt their radiance long after the doors closed.

❧

A cacophony of horns shattered his reflections, and he realized that all of the cars had been moving except his. He apologized to the petulant drivers behind him with a wave of his hand, picked up speed, and joined the flow of traffic heading back into the city.

9 781947 521759